WE DIDN'T MEAN TO START A SCHOOL

*For Lucy and Monica with lots of love.
I would like to thank Eric Hester,
John Phillips and Alison Birkett
for their advice, encouragement and help.*

WE DIDN'T MEAN
TO START A SCHOOL

A FOUR WINDS STORY

JULIA BLYTHE

First published in 1998

Gracewing
Fowler Wright Books
2 Southern Avenue, Leominster
Herefordshire
HR6 0QF

ISBN 0 85244 477 X

Typesetting by Action Typesetting Ltd,
Gloucester, GL1 1SP

Printed by Redwood Books
Trowbridge, Wiltshire BA14 8RN

Chapter 1

It all began with a family crisis. It was to turn into a most splendid adventure, but it didn't feel like that at the time.

Mr Brown had been given an important new job which meant that the whole family would be moving to a different part of Britain. The prospect was very exciting and Geraldine and Jeannie, the twelve year old twins, had excitedly learned about their new home in Cornwall, a new school, and the beautiful countryside. The three smaller children – Georgie, Timothy, and Benjamin – were too young to take in much about the changes.

Their old home was sold. In January a whole new life would begin. They all went to Grandma's for a few days. This in itself was fun because Grandma's small house was almost bursting at the seams with all of them and there would be even more when Aunt Win and Uncle Harry came to visit.

The two girls lay in bed and talked. Jeannie wriggled her toes pleasurably against her hot water bottle and felt the tingling warmth go all through her. She wasn't going to admit it to Geraldine, who always seemed so confident, but she wasn't altogether keen on the idea of all the changes. She was rather sorry to be leaving their old school and all their friends. The twins' very best friend was Amanda, who lived near them and was sometimes teasingly called the 'extra twin' by the other girls because, having no brothers and sisters of her own, she loved spending time with the Browns and sharing in their games and talk and secrets.

'I'm going to miss Amanda and all our other chums at St Catherine's,' she said doubtfully, still snuggling down into the warmth and enjoying the chance to talk.

'I'm sure the new school will be loads of fun,' said Geraldine. 'Didn't Mummy say she was taking us shopping next week to get our uniforms?'

'Yes.' Jeannie was sleepy and cosy. 'Doesn't it feel funny to think of all our own ordinary things whizzing their way, even perhaps at this moment, down to Cornwall in a big lorry? Not just our clothes, I mean, but all our books and toys and everything.'

'We're between-times,' said Geraldine, thinking about it. 'Not quite in the old life, and not yet in the new one. Everything's up for changing, everything's waiting for the new chapter.'

And then the next day the bombshell came. Mr Brown received a telephone call from his new office, summoning him to an important meeting. He was rather cross at having to leave the family party just when they were all enjoying themselves but it couldn't be helped. It was very snowy. He pulled on his boots to make his way out to the car and they all helped to dig it out and put ashes down in the road and see him safely off on the journey into London. A bit later he telephoned.

'Daddy sounded rather bewildered,' said Mrs Brown, coming back into the kitchen where the girls were helping their grandmother make a batch of biscuits for their Aunt Win's visit at teatime. 'He says there are some changes of plan, and rather exciting news about the new job, and he's hurrying home now to tell us all about it. He said to be sure to have the kettle on, as we'd all need a cup of tea. In fact he said to make his a brandy!'

After that, of course, they could hardly wait until he got home, and when they heard him at the door the girls rushed out in front of their little brothers to be the first to greet their father and bombard him with questions.

'A major crisis has blown up in Japan,' Mr Brown explained over tea, 'and the firm has asked me to go and help sort it out. I said I couldn't, of course, because of the family, and they said immediately that my wife could go with me. It'll mean enormous changes of plans all round, of course. There's the house in Cornwall.'

'The house in Cornwall can wait for us,' said Mrs Brown. 'We can rent it out if necessary, until we come back again. The main thing is to keep the family together. But what on earth are we going to do about everything? A place to live in, schools for the children, travel arrangements.'

Mr Brown put his arm round her. 'One thing at a time old girl,' he said. 'We'll sort everything out. They want me to go to Japan right away. But I've told them that I can't go until I've made some domestic arrangements. If you're all game to give it a go, let's all see if we can make it work.'

He tried to make it all sound fun, but he was worried. What about schooling for the girls? His wife would have her hands full with three little boys to organise in a strange country, to say nothing of establishing a new home and having all their goods shipped out there.

Just at that moment came a knock on the door. Aunt Win! They had almost forgotten her. Grandma bustled out into the hall to greet her.

'Winifred dear! Lovely to see you, and you've arrived at such an exciting moment. All the family are here and there's talk of them going to Japan! Do get warm. The kettle's on.'

What a lot of news there was to tell! It was quite a long time before Aunt Win digested all of it, and then she was finally allowed to tell her own news.

'Well, I think it's extraordinary!' she said with astonishment. 'I came here all ready to break some remarkable news to you, and now I find you've beaten me to it and my own news sounds quite tame!'

'What is it?' 'Do tell us?' 'Is it about Uncle Harry?' Everyone asked questions at once.

'No, it's not about Harry, well, only indirectly. He'll be joining us later. But it's through him that this new house has come into our hands.' Aunt Win tried to tell the story properly, but kept getting interrupted. Her husband, Uncle Harry, was a distinguished soldier, more than once decorated for bravery, something of a hero to the younger members of the family, a tall, good-looking suntanned man with dark brown eyes and jet-black hair. Usually, any adventures in the family might be expected to have happened to him. He had travelled around the world and now held an important position in the Ministry of Defence which still involved him in flying off to adventures in distant places.

'Tell us about the house. What house is it? Is it in England?'

'Well, it's simply this: an elderly relation of Harry's died recently. She was his great-aunt, I think, but they hardly ever saw each other. She owned an hotel, rather a nice one, out in the country. Shortly before she died, it was closed. A new motorway was built nearby and people stopped wanting to stay there. But the building itself is still in very good shape, and in her will she left it all to him. There are no debts, a little bit of money in the bank, and this great big place which isn't any use for an hotel any more and is honestly much too big for us to live in.' Aunt Win rummaged in her bag and produced photographs. It was a splendid old-style house, set in pleasant grounds, with a tennis-court and wooded gardens. There were some brochures, too: 'Come to Four Winds – a delightful old-style country hotel offering a warm welcome. Open log fires in the drawing-room, good home-cooking, pleasant views, each room with private bathroom.'

'What on earth will you do with it?' asked Jeannie. It seemed impossible to imagine Uncle Harry settling into a quiet country hotel. He and Aunt Win had a small flat in London which was quite adequate for all their needs.

'I haven't got the least idea,' said Aunt Win. 'I tell you what, though, you can help us to decide. I'm going there to visit in a few days, and we'll all take a look around and see what we should do with the old place.'

'Well, if we can't go to Japan with you, Daddy, some of us will just have to go and live in Aunt Win's new house in the country!' joked Geraldine.

'I haven't told you all the other bits of news,' said Aunt Win. 'It gets more complicated. Uncle Harry's off again shortly on one of his jaunts, and I'd planned to go and do some more language work in Switzerland.' They all nodded. Some years ago, before she had met Uncle Harry, Aunt Win had been working at a girls' school in Switzerland. It was an international academy where she had taught English and had taken the opportunity herself to become fluent in French and German. She still went abroad occasionally to work as a teacher, and sometimes took private pupils when at home.

'I'd got it all organised, and two girls I was going to teach in Switzerland are expecting me there for a term of extra private coaching,' she said. 'I don't like to let them down. Short of inviting them here to Britain, I can't see any way out of it. I'm committed to giving them some lessons for the next three months – halfway up a Swiss mountain!'

Grandma was busy cutting cake and passing it round. 'It seems an awful waste to let that lovely hotel stay closed up and cold all through the winter,' she said.

'Well, I can't really fly home from Switzerland just to look after an empty hotel,' Aunt Win started to say, and then the doorbell rang again and it was Uncle Harry. He blew into the dining-room with gusts of cold air, threw his delighted small nephews into the air, kissed all the females in the room with great enthusiasm, dug in his pockets and produced huge quantities of golden chocolate coins, and then sat for a big mug of tea. Everyone started to tell him excitedly about Japan.

'The worst thing is that I'll be left all alone in England, with no one to visit me,' lamented Grandma. 'Win in Switzerland, you flying off to goodness knows where, and then all the rest of the family in Japan. I'll miss you all terribly. And Japan,' she suddenly added seriously, 'is no place to try to organise these girls' education. Surely you'll have to try to do something about that?'

'Simple, really, if only we organised ourselves properly,' said Jeannie, not really thinking about what she was saying. 'Aunt Win's got a big house and is going to be all alone while Uncle Harry's away. She knows all about teaching. Why don't Geraldine and I stay with her and have lessons there until Mummy and Daddy organise things in Japan?'

'Oh, do let's!' cried Geraldine enthusiastically.

'And the two girls from Switzerland leave their mountainside and hurry over here to join you, I suppose?' laughed Mrs Brown.

'Well, why not?' asked Uncle Harry. 'Sounds a good plan to me. It's taken care of the next three months, anyway. I don't like to think of Win being all alone in that great old hotel and she's tired of travelling to foreign places. Let the Swiss girls join her in Britain, if they're that keen, and she can take care of your girls all at the same time.'

5

Of course there was a great deal more talk after that – about Japan, and how soon things could be organised, and whether or not the girls going with Aunt Win was a mad plan or not. And later, much later, when the children had all gone to bed, the Brown parents and Aunt Win and Uncle Harry sat earnestly round the table and looked at plans and diaries and talked about arrangements and possibilities.

It all took a lot of talking and several mugs of tea and lots of cheerful enthusiasm, and the more they talked, the more the idea of using Four Winds as a base for the two girls while the rest of the family went to Japan made more and more sense. And the final result was that, the next morning, Mr Brown telephoned his firm to say that he'd accept the new job in Japan, provided his wife and three smallest children could fly out immediately to join him. And Geraldine and Jeannie found that they were looking forward, not to a new school in Cornwall, but to something entirely different – a big old hotel in the countryside, with Aunt Win and possibly two other girls from Switzerland!

Chapter 2

In all the excitement Geraldine and Jeannie had almost forgotten that their great friend Amanda was coming to spend the day with them on New Year's Eve. This had been planned as a grand farewell before the family departed for Cornwall but now, of course, they had all the new plans to tell her, and it was two very talkative and excited twins who greeted her at the front door when she arrived at Grandma's cottage. To make things easier, Amanda was to stay overnight with her cousin who lived not far away, so the girls could have a full day together.

'Our parents are going to Japan, and we're going to stay with our aunt at a sort of old hotel in the country!' began Geraldine eagerly.

'And two girls from Switzerland, who don't speak English very well, are going to fly out to join us!' added Jeannie, for this new addition to the plans had now been organised, with Marie Dubois and Evangeline Schratt due to arrive in England in the second week of January.

'You can hardly move in this house without someone rushing to the telephone or sitting making lists,' grinned Geraldine. 'Mummy's looking at brochures about Japan, and endlessly telephoning removal companies and telling them to leave different boxes of things in different places. Jeannie's and my clothes, and some of our books and bits and pieces, are to come with us to Aunt Win's. All the proper furniture from our old house is going into store in Cornwall, near the house we've bought but aren't now using. And some of the things are going with Mummy and Daddy and the little ones to Japan. Meanwhile, we're all based here at Grandma's, which I suppose is sort of home for us all until we've got official addresses somewhere else!'

When Geraldine and Jean had been born, their names had been chosen because, as twins, they could be Gerry and Jeannie. But Geraldine had made clear, once she got older, that she disliked the shortened form of her name and wanted to be the full Geraldine. In this, as in so many other things, the twins, although very good friends and very fond of one another, were very different. They were not identical twins, although they were often dressed alike and enjoyed being a little team together. Geraldine was slightly taller than Jeannie and was the more talkative of the two. She liked organising things and taking the lead in various projects. Jeannie was quieter, gained higher marks at school, and sometimes unexpectedly came up with better ideas than Geraldine, or improved on her original plans. Her dark straight hair was in two shining plaits, an old-fashioned style which suited her well, while Geraldine's short wavy hair had more than a hint of auburn in it, echoed in the freckles which were sprinkled liberally across her nose. The two girls rarely quarrelled and, although each had her own hobbies – Jeannie was good at skating while Geraldine preferred team sports such as hockey and netball – they were happy to spend much of their leisure time together.

They led Amanda upstairs to their own small den on the landing, where they could sit on the beds and gossip comfortably.

At first the twins were so eager to tell their news, and to chatter about Japan and Four Winds and all the new things that were about to happen, that they failed to notice Amanda's mood. Then Jeannie realised that their friend had not been saying very much.

'Well, what's up with you?' she said at last. 'Did you have a good Christmas? You seem a bit quiet.'

'Oh, I'm all right,' said Amanda with a slight sigh. 'And yes, I had an absolutely super Christmas. My parents gave me a wonderful toboggan and I've been whizzing down the hill with it – you know, Corney Hill, near the school, just round the corner from where I live. But I s'pose I'm just feeling a bit gloomy, thinking about January, and going back to school, and you not being there and everything suddenly being dull.' She sat picking at the counterpane for a moment. 'And my cousin's feeling gloomy too,' she added as a sudden after-thought.

'Your cousin? Why? I didn't know you were specially friendly with her anyway,' said Geraldine. 'Isn't she much older than you?'

'Mmm, yes. In fact we don't really know each other very well,' said Amanda thoughtfully. 'But I arrived there yester-day afternoon and Uncle Jim and Auntie Mary – her parents, you know – gave us a super tea and then we sat up late talking. She's an only child like me and somehow we found we'd got lots in common. She's nearly sixteen, which seems awfully grown up in lots of ways, but it's really only three and a half years older than us. And she simply hates the school she's at. Most of the girls there are crazy about pop music and she really likes classical stuff. Her father, Uncle Jim, is a concert pianist and plays most beautifully. He played a bit for us yesterday evening. And her mother sings and used to travel around a lot to concerts. Alison's rather a quiet girl. She's nice. I feel awfully sorry for her, because she's really dreading going back to school. There's a bunch of girls who started to pick on her last term and told her that in the New Year they'd really make her life a misery. They've decided she's too old-fashioned. One of them actually slashed at her new blazer last term and made a great hole in it because they said she always looked too neat and tidy.'

The twins looked at Amanda thoughtfully. Bullying was horrible, and they had seen just enough of it at their own old school to know what it was like.

'How horrible for her,' said Geraldine. 'Can't you do some-thing to cheer her up, at least to give her a really good time these holidays?'

'She seemed pleased with the present I'd brought her, anyway,' said Amanda, 'it was a book about horses. She's crazy about them. Mummy and I chose the book together. Mummy's her godmother. I did think, actually, of telling Mummy all about Alison when I got home, to see if she could talk to Alison's mum and see what could be done about the bullying. Alison hasn't said much to her parents because she doesn't want them to think she's a cry-baby.'

The talk turned to other things, and presently the twins found themselves enthusing to Amanda about Four Winds and showing her some of Aunt Win's brochures. 'Of course, it won't be like an hotel when we get there,' said Jeannie. 'It's all been closed down and will just be like an ordinary private house. But there's a couple living there, Mr and Mrs Drummond, who look after the place and haven't got anywhere else to go. All the other staff have left, of course. Aunt Win wants to keep Mr and Mrs Drummond on, as there's so much to be done just to keep the house clean and the gardens organised.'

'Aunt Win's there today, as a matter of fact,' said Geraldine. She's with Uncle Harry, sorting things out and deciding which rooms to use and so on. I must say it all sounds very grand – beautiful big bedrooms, each one with a television and private bathroom! I can't wait.'

'I think all the televisions will be removed, if I know Aunt Win,' said Jeannie wisely. 'I don't think she's going to treat us to life in a luxury hotel. I heard her telling Mummy that she'll try to make it into a comfortable, homey sort of place and that the real difficulty will be keeping it all heated. I think the expense is worrying her a bit.'

'She ought to take some more pupils in, just to help pay for it all,' suggested Amanda.

'Hey, wait a minute, she isn't running it as a school!' cried Jeannie.

'Isn't she?' retorted Amanda. 'It sounds like one to me. Two nieces, both going there because she's going to teach them while their parents are in Japan. Two girls arriving from Switzerland. What do you call that except a school?'

Then suddenly all three girls had the same idea. All at once, as brilliant ideas do, it flashed into their minds and was there, fizzing with life, right in front of them.

'Let's turn it into a proper school, Amanda!' breathed Geraldine.

'Just what I thought!' said Jeannie. 'Four Winds School! A proper one, with us as the founders, Aunt Win as the head, and everything planned just the way we want it!'

'My idea too!' said Amanda at the same time. 'I'm going there! Just listen! I'm going to go home tomorrow and get my parents to telephone your Aunt Win the very first thing!'

After that, things started to happen very quickly. The girls spent the rest of the day chattering and planning. The next day saw an amazing amount of telephoning. Amanda's mother telephoned Mrs Brown to ask about 'this mad idea of my girl about some school your girls' aunt is planning'. Amanda's cousin Alison pleaded with her parents to get in touch and start talking about it all too. Telephone calls went to Aunt Win at Four Winds, who telephoned Uncle Harry at their London flat and told him that a crazy but delightful project was taking shape. He was busy making arrangements for an Army expedition to a distant region of Africa and was absolutely delighted that Aunt Win would be kept happy and busy in his absence. 'Let the school flourish as big as you like!' he said generously. 'Only thing I ask is, make sure the girls learn some cookery, and keep a comfortable corner for me when I get home! I'd like a really special meal, please, cooked for me by all of you when I get home!'

And so the Four Winds project, which had begun as an emergency measure just to care for Jeannie and Geraldine until things were ready for them in Japan, had become, in the space of a few days, a fully-grown project which was turning into – no, Aunt Win wouldn't let them use the word 'school'.

'It's not a school,' she kept insisting when Jeannie and Geraldine were sitting with her at Grandma's kitchen table, working out various details. 'Don't run away with big ideas. This is just a temporary arrangement for you and the Swiss girls, and your friends Amanda and Alison while it suits them. We'll have a few months together and then gradually you'll all go on to other places. It won't be registered as a school. I'm just giving private lessons to a small group of girls. I'm taking Amanda because she wants to be with you, and because her parents don't feel she'll be happy at your old school without you and Alison is coming because of the bullying.' She paused and looked at the names on the list in front of her. 'I must admit it will be useful to have Alison,' she said. 'She seems a very pleasant, responsible girl, and it's good to have someone rather older. The two Swiss girls are about twelve.

So we'll have quite a wide age range on our hands.'

But privately, Jeannie and Geraldine, Amanda and Alison, all talked and thought about 'Four Winds School' and never really considered calling the arrangement anything else.

Plans now went along smoothly. Aunt Win would take Jeannie and Geraldine to Four Winds by train, collecting Alison and Amanda on the way. Once they were settled at Four Winds, the Swiss girls would arrive by air, and Aunt Win would drive out to the airport to greet them. Lessons would include French and German, both of which Aunt Win spoke fluently, together with mathematics and science which would be a taught by a teacher friend who had been looking for some part-time work. A lady would be travelling in to give Alison her music lessons as Four Winds boasted a particularly fine piano. Other arrangements would have to be made in the first few days as people got settled. Aunt Win had noticed an announcement about ballet classes in the nearby village, which she thought the girls would enjoy, and she was also determined that her pupils would study Latin, something, about which Geraldine and Jeannie were decidedly less than enthusiastic. History and geography would be taught as a matter of course, and text books, exercise books, a black-board and various other items of equipment were already being obtained. The first few days of term would clearly be spent helping to make sure that all functioned smoothly. Following Uncle Harry's advice, cookery was to be on the curriculum. 'We'll all have to help out if we're to eat prop-erly,' Aunt Win pointed out. 'Mrs Drummond will be kept busy doing the cooking and getting the washing done. I'll draw up a kitchen rota and everyone must take a turn at all the various tasks. We'll make it fun and all help each other.'

Aunt Win was a born organiser. It had been a great sadness to herself and Harry that they had had no children of their own, and the various teaching posts she had held at foreign schools had been interesting but had not really used up all her talents. Now, slowly awakening, she felt a sense of what was to be a great project. Carefully setting aside a couple of rooms for her own and her husband's private use, she arranged things at Four Winds to accommodate the six girls who were to be her pupils, with a pleasant airy room as a schoolroom and a cosy room with a big fireplace as the girls' own common-room where they could relax.

There was no need to buy desks, cupboards or other equipment. A couple of large tables from the hotel's restaurant turned what had been an upstairs lounge into a pleasant schoolroom. Everyone would work comfortably together rather than sitting in formal rows. As Jeannie had predicted, all private telephones and televisions were moved. Another room was set aside as a library. The hotel already had up-to-date computers. Aunt Win established a downstairs room as her study and installed the telephone there, together with her own desk for administrative work. In what had been the hotel's entrance foyer, a big welcoming fire would burn in a grate. Books and pictures from the London flat, and some of the Brown family's furniture that could not be stored elsewhere, helped to make a homelike atmosphere.

The days sped by swiftly. The Japan plans all went ahead smoothly, and more quickly than it could possibly have been imagined, Mr and Mrs Brown, with their small sons, were organised with a little flat waiting for them in the city's centre near the office where Mr Brown would be working. Mrs Brown worried that the girls might be distressed at the thought of the family being in different places, but in fact they were so excited at the thought of being at Four Winds and inventing a whole new school, that saying farewell to their parents for a few months didn't seem particularly hard.

It was only when they actually came to say goodbye, and waved them off at the airport, that it all suddenly felt rather serious. It would be Easter before they all met again, either in Japan or at Grandma's.

Chapter 3

The next day began with an early telephone call from Aunt Win.

'This is getting too ridiculous!' her brisk voice crackled down the line to Grandma. 'I've suddenly acquired two more pupils! And the trouble is, I can't very well say no to them because their mother is the extremely nice woman who's volunteered to come here to teach geography. She's a widow and coping with the girls on her own. We're all rather snowed up here, and the prospect of driving the girls out to the big local school several miles away once term began was rather getting her down. I suggested in a weak moment that, just for a short while, the girls could come here for lessons, and she leaped at it. Apparently one of the girls had not been particularly happy at school and is keen on the idea of a change. The other is rather reluctant. We'll just have to see how things work out.'

Grandma gave the twins a good breakfast and then whisked them away for a last-minute shopping expedition. They needed toothpaste and soap and some extra pairs of tights, but she also wanted them to choose something each as a leaving-present.

'In this cold weather, what you both really need is woolly hats,' she said doubtfully. 'And warm scarves, too. With a name like Four Winds it sounds to me as though the grounds of that place are going to be pretty cold when you go out at playtime.' Jeannie had never liked bobble-hats and was instead eyeing a rack of bright berets. She chose a scarlet one and put it on.

'How does it look?' she asked, grinning at herself in the mirror. She liked the cheerful look of the girl who grinned back at her, dark plaits bobbing with excitement as she turned her head from side to side.

'I'll have one that matches it!' said Geraldine, after first picking up a blue beret and then settling for a red one like Jeannie's. 'It's fun being dressed alike. I like these. Are they very expensive, Grandma? Could we have them?'

Grandma beamed, enjoying the sight of the twins. The price was very reasonable. 'Scarves to match too?' she asked. Five minutes later they were proudly wearing their matching scarlet outfits. They thanked Grandma with enthusiastic hugs as they hurried out to the car.

While they were doing their final packing at home, Amanda and Alison arrived, looking suddenly self-conscious with bulging suitcases containing all the things they might need for the weeks ahead. They joined the twins for cups of steaming coffee at Grandma's kitchen table and were soon gossiping happily about Four Winds and future plans.

Grandma looked at the clock. 'Your Aunt Win will be here in about an hour,' she said. 'I've got a list here of last-minute things that might have been forgotten, and I'd like to check it with you before you close your cases. Oh, and here are your sandwiches.'

It was exciting doing all the last-minute things. 'Toothbrush, washing-bag, hot-water bottle,' Grandma read from her list. 'Something to read on the train? And the school things we bought yesterday, pencils and notebooks.'

After she had bustled downstairs with some of the luggage there was a quiet moment when the four girls were alone on the landing.

'Listen,' said Geraldine urgently, 'this is the beginning of it – Four Winds School. Let's make a private promise now, a really solemn one, that whatever Aunt Win says, this really will be a proper school, and we'll all make it a happy one, so we can stick together and turn it into something really successful.'

'Yes, definitely,' said Jeannie. 'I want to be the first to promise. Four Winds will be our very own school and we'll make it everything a really good school should be.'

15

'I promise, too,' said Alison. 'This will be a school where everything can begin today from a fresh start. No bullying. No sneering at anyone. Our very own school.'

'I promise that Four Winds will be the best and happiest school in England,' said Amanda. 'It's a school that began simply because the four founding pupils said it should. Let's all make it a big success.'

'The Four Winds promise,' said Geraldine solemnly. 'We'll be loyal to Aunt Win and to one another.'

And with that they all trooped downstairs.

Funnily enough, perhaps because they had made a promise to take the school seriously, even though Aunt Win didn't know about it, there was a distinctly organised atmosphere among the group when Aunt Win arrived half an hour later. They all greeted her rather formally and she seemed glad that they had a business-like approach. Using Grandma's car, they were ferried to the station in two groups, and then all finally gathered by the ticket office. Grandma kissed her two granddaughters good-bye affectionately. She was sorry to see them go, but also quite glad at the prospect of a few days' rest. Her small cottage had been crowded for a long time and there was a good bit of housework to be done. She checked that the girls had their sandwiches and all their luggage, gave them further warm hugs and was gone. That was the last link with Christmas and the holidays. Now the term was beginning. As the train drew in, the four girls got in, chattering excitedly, while Aunt Win, looking more and more like a headmistress, fussed around with the suitcases and the tickets.

'Tell us about the two new girls, Aunt Win,' said Jeannie eagerly, once they were all settled in the carriage. Already it seemed quite normal to be using the school expression 'new girls', although the school had hardly opened yet and every girl was just as 'new' as any other.

'Well, it happened quite by accident,' said Aunt Win, laying down the newspaper she had been about to read, and looking round at the cheerful faces. 'I was speaking to Mrs Hurry – yes, that's her name, your geography teacher – and of course we got chatting about the weather and all this snow, and she was telling me what a nuisance it would be to

16

get her two girls into Mentlesham, the nearest big town, to school every morning. Unfortunately the buses are terribly unreliable at the moment, and apparently the girls were in constant trouble last term for being late. One of them – Elizabeth, the older girl – also seems to have got into rather a silly crowd at school, and failed most of her exams, so her mother's rather worried that she's making a mess of things, and the younger one, Joan, has been in bed for a week with a dreadful cold. One way and another I found myself saying, "Well, why not bring them along to lessons at Four Winds for a few weeks, to see how it goes?" So there we are. Two more pupils. With Marie and Evangeline arriving the day after tomorrow, we look all set for quite a big school. Except,' she added hurriedly, 'that it's not a school, just a convenient private arrangement. Don't let's start talking as if we'd got an enormous invention on our hands.'

Her four pupils exchanged sidelong glances as she returned to her newspaper. There were secret grins. Whatever their headmistress said, Four Winds was a school anyway, and the pupils were steadily arriving!

At the main London terminus, Aunt Win suddenly became very headmistress-like indeed. 'Keep together girls,' she said briskly. 'I don't want any of you getting lost. And keep your luggage with you and be responsible for it. Don't just stand there dreaming, Jeannie dear, we've all got to stay together or we'll get muddled on the Underground.'

'Oh my goodness,' she said a moment later to Amanda, 'I do wish you were all wearing red berets like my two nieces. I'm trying to keep you all in view but it would make life so very much easier if you were all wearing something more distinctive. Then I could pick you all out in a crowd.'

'Just what I was thinking!' interrupted Alison. 'Jeannie and Geraldine are dressed alike, as usual, because they're twins, and Amanda and I feel rather out of things. Also my head's cold. My mother gave me some spending-money. Can I go into that shop and buy red berets for Amanda and me? That way we'd match the others, and you'd find it easier all round.'

It was a sensible idea, and before Aunt Win could think of a reason why not, Alison had dived off into the shop, emerging with bright red berets and scarves, the same cheerful cherry-colour as the twins were wearing. Amid a certain amount of preening in shop windows, she and Amanda put them on. The whole effect was rather delightful and made the girls giggle as they trailed along with their luggage.

'Well, I must say it does make it easier to count,' Aunt Win admitted as she surveyed them all when they arrived at the Underground station. 'And you do all look very nice. I suppose you don't want me to wear a red beret too?' They all assured her that this wasn't necessary. Once on the Underground, they were all too busy organising luggage to worry about much else, and then came the transfer to another train and the final journey down to Four Winds.

'Mr Drummond is meeting us at the station,' said Aunt Win. 'He's got a van with seats in the back, and plenty of room for all our luggage. He will have been to the town too, to pick up supplies for the next week. His wife's a very good cook, incidentally. Uncle Harry and I have been simply wallowing in the most delicious food.'

Her reference to Uncle Harry brought up the problem of what Amanda and Alison were to call him. He wasn't an uncle of theirs, and nor was Aunt Win their aunt. And the problem was further complicated by the fact that Harry and Win had a very comic and uncomfortably suitable surname. It was 'Battle'. Jeannie and Geraldine, along with all the rest of the family, had always delighted in having an uncle who was not only a courageous soldier but even had a surname that indicated as much! They had liked introducing him as 'This is my uncle, Major Battle' and giggling. But now Amanda and Alison faced having to greet him and use the name without dissolving into helpless laughter. And what about addressing Aunt Win? Saying 'Good morning, Mrs Battle' to your teacher each day was somehow going to be impossible without giggles. And imagine saying 'This is my head-teacher, Mrs Win Battle'! Amanda grinned as she thought of it. A suitable name for a lady fighting to start a new school! But should she just call her 'Aunt Win', as Geraldine and Jeannie did?

The problem had to be shelved for the time being. All else was forgotten in the excitement of craning forward to catch the first glimpse of the place that was to be their home for the next few weeks – Four Winds School.

It stood back from the road, a large house built in mock-tudor manor style that actually dated only from the 1930s. Its white pebble-dashed walls were relieved by large black-painted wooden gables, and there were mullioned windows winking in the winter sunshine. A short straight drive led up to the front door which was flanked by conifer trees, now laden with heavy snow. On either side of the drive, the garden lawns were immaculate. No footprints had broken the crisp white snow which also covered a sundial, a bird-table and several wooden seats and what looked like a small summer-house.

'It's pretty, isn't it?' asked Aunt Win approvingly, as a chorus of 'Oohs' greeted this first sight of the house. The van crunched its way up the drive through tracks already made in the snow, and then the front door opened and a smiling person, who could only be Mrs Drummond, appeared greeting them all in a friendly way and making everyone suddenly feel that they had arrived at home, rather than at some strange new place.

'Welcome, welcome to Four Winds,' she cried with a wide open-arm gesture. 'Oh, it's lovely to be greeting guests again and to know that the rooms will be filled. Just like old times, except that you're rather young hotel guests! What happy faces! You're all smiling and cheerful. But you must be cold. John'll help you with your cases and I've got hot chocolate waiting for you all to drink right here by the hall fire.'

Mr Drummond – John to his wife – was silently but cheerily lifting cases out of the car and the girls were soon busy helping him. Then, pulling off their red hats and scarves and peeling off coats and gloves, they were holding their hands out to the fire and looking all round them.

'And this is where I say a proper welcome to you all, too,' said Aunt Win, turning from the mirror where she'd been tidying herself. 'This is your home for the next few weeks, girls, and I hope it will be a very happy one. Harry and I are just delighted to have you all here, and we'll make this into a really cheerful place to work together. Let's drink to our success in hot chocolate!'

And so, over steaming mugs of chocolate with whipped

cream on top, Four Winds School really came into being. Soon Uncle Harry came whistling into the hall and shook hands with Amanda and Alison, hugged his two nieces, telling them all with obvious pleasure that it was really good to have them there. 'This place is horribly big for just Win and myself and the Drummonds,' he said. 'Feels most peculiar just rattling about in it. Now you're here, we can make the place feel like something worthwhile. I'm off to Africa in a few weeks so you won't see much of me after that. Look after Winifred for me, won't you girls, and make sure she keeps happy and cheerful?'

They all liked him, and a chorus of cheerful promises answered him. 'That's all right then,' he said, rubbing his hands together. 'Well, I'm a bit busy until lunch, so I'll see you then.'

Once they were warm through after their journey, there came the excitement of exploring the house and seeing the rooms where they were to sleep.

'I didn't think you'd like to be miles away from each other in this big building,' said Aunt Win, 'although it's not so very vast when you get to know it. Actually by hotel standards it's really rather small. But I chose this big front room for you three younger girls and there's a smaller room off it, with a bit more privacy, for Alison.' She led the way into a sunny cheerful room, with a light rose-sprinkled wallpaper. Three single beds, each with a chair and a cupboard beside it, were the main furniture, and there was a small central table with a lamp on it and a pretty posy of dried flowers. There were plenty of large cupboards and some bookshelves. It all had the rather formal air of an hotel bedroom but it was warm and welcoming. Alison was entranced with her own small room, which had the same attractive wallpaper.

'If you'd like to unpack and make yourselves at home here, we'll continue the tour in about ten minutes,' said Aunt Win. 'Hang things up in the wardrobes and leave your suitcases out on the landing. We'll stack them in one of the big cupboards downstairs. You'll have to choose which bed you each want, and no squabbling! Toss a coin for it if necessary. Oh, and this is your bathroom, with a shower, you see and stacks of hot water. You hang the towels here. There's an extra washbasin in the room, too, which should make life easier.'

'I'd like the bed by the window, please!' said Amanda quickly, before anyone else could lay any claim. Jeannie's face fell because she'd had her eye on that one, too. She started to say something but Geraldine butted in, 'Well, I'll have this bed here, then,' swinging her suitcase up on to it. That left no choice at all for Jeannie, which didn't seem quite fair.

'Hey, suppose I want it?' she demanded and went over to the bed, as if to inspect it and see for herself if it suited her.

'Well, I've already chosen ...' began Geraldine.

'And I did claim the bed by the window first,' said Amanda, raising her voice just in case there should be any arguing.

'I'm all right, anyway, as I've got a room all to myself!' sang out Alison rather smugly, swinging past them and giving her head a slight toss as she did so.

'Oh, who cares about what silly bed anyone gets anyway?' said Geraldine, loudly and rather sulkily, pushing Jeannie aside and sitting down on the one she had chosen. 'I got in first with that one so that's that.' Jeannie instantly gave her a shove, which she returned, and suddenly the situation developed into one of their rare quarrels, with both of them shouting and Amanda joining in to defend her own choice of bed, and Alison bellowing 'I think you're all being incredibly childish!' from the next-door room. This only had the effect of making everyone shout even louder, with Alison joining in herself and insults flying about. And then suddenly, in the middle of it, the door slammed noisily and there was Aunt Win, looking cross and rather astonished.

'Really girls!' she said in a clear and carrying voice. 'I can't have this at all. Be quiet! Be quiet immediately!'

She was a teacher. Her voice carried authority with immediate effect and the shouting stopped, although the faces still glared. 'If you're going to argue,' said Aunt Win, 'I'll close down Four Winds immediately, send the twins back to their grandmother and you girls to your parents. You can each have the bed nearest to where you are now standing. No, my word is final. And I'm going to watch while you unpack, and you're going to do it in complete silence, because I'm not

21

going to have the pleasant atmosphere of this house spoiled by a lot of silly girls quarrelling.'

There was a tense moment as each girl looked at the bed nearest her and then, with a shrug, Geraldine opened her suitcase and rather sulkily got out her nightdress. Aunt Win's ruling left Amanda still with the window bed and Geraldine with the one she had chosen, while Jeannie got the bed nearest the door. Alison put on a smug smile as she turned to go to her own small room but Aunt Win stopped her. 'No,' she said, 'not with that expression on your face, please. You've all got a very nice place to sleep in, and no one is going to look superior. Just quickly and quietly get on with your unpacking, and I'm watching you to notice any horrid sneer or unpleasantness.'

The atmosphere was rather grim as each girl started to unpack her case but no one dared to disobey Aunt Win and break the silence. She stood and watched as the cases were emptied and the girls piled things into drawers and cupboards. When it was almost completed she clapped her hands. 'Right,' she said, 'you can talk now, and the first thing you're going to do is shake hands and tell each other you're sorry. There's not going to be any quarrelling at Four Winds and everyone must always forgive each other. Shake now – that's right, each of you to the other. And as you come out, you must each of you shake hands with me.'

They all felt slightly silly doing that but it did break the tense atmosphere, and as they left the room each was actually quite happy with the bed she had been allocated. Jeannie had discovered while unpacking that hers was nearest to the light switch, which could be reached quite easily without getting out of bed, giving her an undoubted advantage over the other girls, so perhaps Amanda and Geraldine hadn't been so clever when they rushed in first, after all.

The rest of the house was quickly explored. There was a big sitting-room for the girls' use, a dining-room in which they would all eat together, the schoolroom where lessons would be held, and a music-room, housing the grand piano. The two girls from Switzerland would have a room to themselves just across the corridor from the English ones. Aunt Win and Uncle Harry were sleeping at the end of the same corridor and could easily be reached during the night if there was any emergency. Everything seemed comfortable and convenient.

From downstairs a bell rang. Mrs Drummond's voice called out, 'I'm sending up the lunch! It's coming in the hatch. Run and look for it!' And sure enough, the dining-room had an old-fashioned pulley system, in which food could be sent up from the kitchen below to arrive most efficiently, piping hot. In a few moments the girls, washed and tidied, were sitting down to an excellent fish pie, with Uncle Harry at one end of the table and Aunt Win at the other, and a lively chatter beginning about all the plans for the days ahead.

Chapter 4

Four Winds had been famous as a comfortable family-style hotel. By the next morning. It seemed as though they had lived there for a long time. Aunt Win had made sure each girl had telephoned to assure her parents that she had arrived safely and settled in. There had been a riotous snowball-fight in the garden at the back of the house – by common agreement it seemed a pity to mess up the beautiful snow at the front – in which Uncle Harry had demonstrated military tactics and showed them how to create an effective ambush. A cheerful supper had been followed by a short 'business meeting' led by Aunt Win.

'Look,' she said, 'I don't want to be too formal about this, and of course we aren't starting lessons till Monday, but I think we ought to be organised. I'm collecting Marie and Evangeline from the airport on Monday afternoon and it might help them if things were already under way by the time they arrive. So let's gather together in the schoolroom at nine on Monday to make a start and talk about the work we're going to do. I've asked Mrs Hurry to bring Elizabeth and Joan here at nine o'clock sharp. She's going to share the teaching with me, as you know, but she won't actually be giving any lessons till Tuesday.' She looked round at the rather serious faces and grinned. 'Tomorrow we'll explore the village and go snowballing, and there's a village pond which looks as though it might be properly frozen. The local Borough Council were sending someone along to test it and put up notices if it's safe for skating. I did tell you to bring skates if you had any, didn't I? And a local firm is going to set up a skate-hire stand anyway.'

'What do we do about breakfast?' asked Alison 'Poor Mrs Drummond seems to be doing a lot of work.'

'That's the next thing we've got to discuss,' said Aunt Win. I'm drawing up a kitchen-help rota. Alison, perhaps you'd help me this evening just to sort out the details? In a big place like this we've all got to take turns to make sure all the work gets done. Remember that in the kitchen, Mrs Drummond is in charge and her word is law. She knows this place better than anyone, so you just do exactly as she says. But she wants your help in planning the menus! Breakfast will be toast and rolls and marmalade, and I'll need two volunteers to help get it ready. I'm the first volunteer. Who'll join me?' She chose Amanda from among the voices that called out, and so the beginning of a routine for meals was established.

After breakfast on Sunday they'd all go to church. 'We're not pagans,' said Aunt Win briskly when Amanda said that surely they hardly needed to go because there'd been quite enough churchgoing over Christmas. 'We've got all week to be busy in, and Sunday morning is the time we give to God. And it's the right way to start our time together here. Let's meet here in the hall at ten o'clock sharp and all walk down together.'

Next day, everyone was ready on time. On an inspiration, Alison decreed that they'd all wear their matching red hats and scarves. Aunt Win grinned when she saw them all, and they all enjoyed the sight of themselves, caught in the mirror as they trooped towards the front door. Uncle Harry grinned too. 'If you don't mind,' he said, 'I think I might sit in a different pew. It's all very jolly, of course, but I feel a bit conspicuous, the only male in this girls' school. So I'll take my prayer-book and bury myself in it a couple of rows behind.'

Mumstone Park, as the small village was called, was a very pretty little place and the girls enjoyed the short walk to church. The priest, Father Higgins, was just unlocking the church as they arrived. He was a tall, energetic young man with a black labrador puppy bounding alongside him. Both priest and dog greeted the group from Four Winds with enthusiasm. Father Higgins had already met Aunt Win and heard about the girls' arrival. He told them they looked smart in their red hats. 'A very jolly colour,' he said. 'I've never understood why some schools choose such depressing colours like black and grey.'

Aunt Win started to say, 'Oh, it's not really a uniform …' but got distracted by the arrival of various other people as the church began to fill up.

The girls shared a couple of hymn-books between them and enjoyed singing the hymns they knew. Aunt Win had been right – this was the proper way to start a new venture together. Alison found herself praying that there'd be no more silly quarrels like the one about choosing the beds. 'And if there are, I won't be the one to make things worse,' she decided. The twins found themselves thinking about their parents, far away in Japan, and asking God to take care of them and watch over all the family.

As they set off again towards Four Winds after leaving the church, Father Higgins came bounding after them, the snow sticking to his long cassock. The puppy, yelping with pleasure, bounded too. Both were a little breathless as they caught up with Aunt Win. 'It's just a thought,' he said. 'Are you serious about taking on any other pupils? It's just that my sister is coming to stay next week. She's thinking of moving to this district and she's got her little girl with her. The child's not been well and hasn't actually been at school for this last term. She's thinking of starting her somewhere new. Perhaps I could mention your school to her? If they find a house they like around here, knowing there's a good school would make all the difference. I think a small and friendly place would suit her.'

Aunt Win laughed, her breath coming out in white puffs in the frosty air. 'Of course she can come!' she said. 'It's becoming a joke. This wasn't meant to be a formal school at all and now it's turning into one! Yes, tell your sister to give me a phone call or just turn up and visit. If she likes what I can offer, I'd love to have another pupil round the schoolroom table. The more the merrier!'

The girls were patting the dog and asking his name. 'It's Canis,' said Father Higgins, and then when the girls looked blank added, 'Latin for dog. You haven't started on Latin yet?' When Jeannie told him they hadn't, and didn't much want to, he laughed. 'Oh, it's not difficult,' he said. 'The important thing is not to make it too serious.' The puppy was friendly and bouncy and energetic like Father Higgins. Jeannie tossed a snowball and Canis bounded off after it. Amanda tossed one at Jeannie as she ran after the dog. Soon all the girls were pelting each other with snow. At first the adults pretended not to notice, then Father Higgins, still talking to Aunt Win, made a quick snowball and caught Geraldine neatly in the middle of her back. She swivelled round to see who had hit her and caught sight of his face, looking solemn and innocent in a very unconvincing way. She quickly mustered snow to pelt him back. He proved a swift and cheerful opponent. Canis bounded about, helping with glee. Things only came to an end when Aunt Win, catching sight of her watch, remembered the need to cook lunch. The group broke up amid much goodwill, and Father Higgins and the puppy – two figures in black and spattered with snow – bounded off together as the Four Winds group made its way back home.

Back at the house, they felt more of a team than ever. 'I'm going to have to draw up an attendance register,' said Aunt Win. 'The four of you, two Swiss girls, Elizabeth and Joan Hurry – yes, I agree it's a funny surname but not half as daft as my own – and now this new child, Father Higgins' niece. Well, I think I'll put you all in alphabetical order and call a register the first morning! And, Alison, if any more pupils arrive I'll turn formal and announce that you're Head Girl!'

Later, talking it all over, the four girls agreed that they rather liked the idea of Alison being Head Girl. Apart from anything else, it meant that she had to take some of the responsibility for organising things. 'You can certainly have the job if you want it, Allie,' said Amanda. 'And we'll all back you up. You've already done the kitchen rota anyway, and the red hats and scarves were your idea too. So you're Head Girl in all but name already!'

Monday morning saw them all waiting quite excitedly in the room that had been set aside for lessons. Sunshine streamed in over the snowy garden and gleamed on the wide table on which some books and papers had been set. The room felt comfortable and organised, but not like a normal classroom. There were warm curtains at the windows and a clock ticked on the graceful mantelpiece. Pictures showed attractive local scenes, and a big arrangement of dried flowers and leaves stood on a corner shelf, its glowing colours making a bright splash of colour against the cream-coloured wall.

Aunt Win came in, leading two rather shy and awkward-looking girls. 'Here we are,' she said. 'This is Elizabeth and this is Joan, and this completes our little group until Marie and Evangeline arrive at the airport this afternoon. Meet your new friends. Here are Alison – she's our oldest girl here – Amanda, and the twins Jeannie and Geraldine. Shake hands and then let's all gather round the table.' For a moment there was a sudden silence round the table as the Four Winds boarders looked at the new day-girls, sizing them up. Then Alison broke the ice with a warm smile and held out her hand. There was a chorus of rather formal 'hallos' as people shook hands.

Elizabeth was a tall, rather sullen-looking girl with very short cropped hair in a slightly 'punk' style. She wore a very short, tight mini-skirt which Amanda found herself thinking must have been very cold in this freezing weather. Elizabeth didn't look particularly happy to be standing in the Four Winds schoolroom and conveyed the impression that she was only there because she had been made to come. She fiddled with one of her large earrings and pushed her hand self-consciously through her stubby hair, looking round the room. Her younger sister, who shared her blonde hair but wore it longer with a softer look, had a pink nose and a slight cough, evidence of what had evidently been a severe cold. She was dressed more warmly in jeans and a thick jersey. She carried a school bag but Elizabeth had just a couple of magazines under her arm.

'Let's start as we mean to go on,' said Aunt Win. 'A proper school has a morning assembly where they have prayers and then someone reads out the notices, but as we're just a small group round the table, we'll have a moment's silence to collect our thoughts and then we'll say the "Our Father" together.' She put her books down quietly on the table and lowered her head. The girls followed her example. After a short silence, Aunt Win's quiet voice led them all in the familiar prayer.

There was a scraping of chairs as they all sat down after the prayer, and then Aunt Win opened the discussion by announcing plans for the day's work.

'I've got the notes and reports and so on from your previous schools,' she said. 'We'll break into two groups in a moment – Elizabeth and Alison, who'll be working on a separate timetable geared to the GCSE syllabus, and then you younger girls, who'll sit at this end of the table I think. We'll start with an English lesson, together because I thought we'd all enjoy doing some Shakespeare together. It's *A Midsummer Night's Dream*, which is the set book for the exam syllabus but which you younger girls will enjoy too. When we've finished with that, I'll have to drive off to the airport to pick up these girls from Switzerland, so I'll leave you some work that you can just do quietly. Over lunch we'll all get to know each other, and then this afternoon a couple of you have got music lessons booked and I'll be doing two lots of French lessons, first with you younger girls and then the older ones.'

In no time, it seemed, they were settling down with books, and Aunt Win was introducing them to the plot of one of Shakespeare's most enjoyable plays. It was then that the girls – all of them, even Elizabeth who was definitely a most reluctant pupil – discovered something very important. Aunt Win was a born teacher. She had the gift of capturing her pupils' attention, making them laugh and enjoy themselves, while opening their minds to the information she was imparting.

They were working under some difficulties because Geraldine and Jeannie had to share one copy of a book between them – a large cumbersome edition of Shakespeare from what had been the hotel's own little library – while Elizabeth and Alison shared the latter's own copy and Amanda and Joan sat either side of Aunt Win to share hers. Outside, the snow had begun to fall again and they couldn't help wanting to look at it, and in any case it felt strange to be sitting round a large glossy table in a room which didn't feel a bit like a traditional classroom. But once they had started reading, the magic of the play came alive. They found themselves engrossed in the plight of the young lovers in the story, and anxious to find out what was going to happen to them. They enjoyed the sound of the words and the beautiful rhythm of them. Aunt Win stopped to explain bits they couldn't understand and encouraged them to ask questions.

The chiming of the clock on the mantelpiece told them it was ten o'clock.

'Time to have a short break and to change pace,' said Aunt Win. 'Now you younger girls, choose one of the passages we've been reading this morning – this speech of Titania is one of the most famous, or this song sung by the fairies as she falls asleep – and copy it out carefully into your exercise books. Then you're going to learn it by heart. Come and show me the piece that you have chosen so that I can check it before you get going. Now, Alison and Elizabeth, I need to sort out some timetabling with you and show you this material to explain the work we really ought to get through over these next few weeks. Can we move across to the other side of the room to give the others some space?'

The mood was businesslike, cheerful and pleasant. It felt comfortable working in the warm room with the snow falling outside. At eleven o'clock Mrs Drummond brought up a tray of hot chocolate and biscuits. This was the signal for a general break, and while Aunt Win made ready to go to the airport, the girls talked and got to know each other. It was agreed that while Aunt Win was out, Alison would explain the kitchen-rota system and other arrangements.

'We're going to have cookery classes twice a week,' she said, still sitting at the big table but with her books pushed aside. It was fun to be starting the adventure of a new school together, sipping chocolate and chatting. 'It's all being planned with Mrs Drummond. There's a fully-equipped kitchen here, with all the latest gadgets, and Mrs Drummond used to cook rather elaborate dinners and lunches for different occasions in the old days. She's got all sorts of top qualifications in catering. In fact, she sometimes gives cookery demonstrations in the local town one night a week, for people who are working to gain formal qualifications, and she said we could gain certificates too if we wanted them.'

'Well, I think it sounds stupid,' said Elizabeth firmly. She was sitting on the table itself, swinging her legs. 'I didn't come here to learn a lot of rubbish about cookery. I won't be staying. It's all just stupid. Quiet, too, and boring. I only came because Mum nagged and nagged and was being a real pain about getting me a lift into school every morning. But coming here instead is just a waste of time.'

Her younger sister looked embarrassed. 'Oh come on, Elizabeth, it's not as bad as all that. It's different, yes, but give it a try. You did promise Mum you'd stick it for a week.'

'There's no rule about keeping promises, is there?' Elizabeth snapped back. 'I think this is all just such a crass idea. I can't think why I ever agreed to come here.'

The mood was distinctly unpleasant and Elizabeth's words cut across the sense of enthusiasm that had been carrying along the other girls. Amanda cleared her throat. 'Well, you can't possibly get into your own school in the town today, at any rate,' she said, putting down her mug and walking over to the window. She looked out at the snow. 'So you may as well give this one a chance, just for a week.' She paused and tried to think of something more friendly to say. 'Tell us about your own school, anyway. Did you enjoy it? Are you missing it?'

Elizabeth looked around the room as if to make sure that Aunt Win was definitely not present and lowered her voice 'Actually, the best thing about it was that you didn't have to do much work if you didn't want to,' she said. 'Some of us used to scoot off a lot of the time. Go into the shopping centre in town and hang about waiting for boys to come and be with us. We'd buy a couple of hamburgers and sit and talk and have a laugh and a cigarette. It was great.'

'Mum guessed you were doing that and had a row with Miss Smith about it,' said Joan. 'That's why she wanted you to come here. It wasn't me that told her,' she added hurriedly. 'I've told you before, I kept my mouth shut. In fact, I really didn't like Mentsham Heights School and I'm glad not to be going there. A lot of girls in my class had started to mess about too, and all they'd ever talk about was boys, and which one they thought was really attractive. I thought they were boring.'

'Well, boys are the most important things, aren't they?' said Elizabeth. 'Who wants to live in a ghastly village where there's no social life? I want discos, music, the chance to go out and about a bit.'

'Have you got a proper boyfriend, then?' asked Alison. She was suddenly feeling lonely. This was what things had been like at her own old school – girls who seemed to be interested only in boys and pop music. She wanted to have a boyfriend too, one day, but only if she met someone who really shared her interests. The idea of hanging round a shopping centre giggling over cigarettes seemed a rather dreary introduction to romance.

'Oh yeah, loads,' said Elizabeth carelessly. 'That's why it's such a waste of time being here. Who needs Shakespeare and that? Boys aren't interested in all that sort of thing.'

'Some are,' said Amanda, suddenly interrupting. 'There's a family that live opposite me at home and they've got two boys a bit older than me who are really super – huge fun and always great to talk to. We met when their parents and mine got together for a barbecue, and since then we've been friends every holidays. I know they're interested in Shakespeare because we all went to an open-air theatre thing once together, when it was held in a local park, and we really enjoyed it. And neither of them like pop music much, though one plays crazy jazz. When I'm ready to have boyfriends, that's the sort of person I'd like. They've got nice manners, too', she added pointedly.

'The sort of boyfriend I'd like,' said Geraldine, who always had a clear-cut point of view about things, 'would be one who was an outdoor type, who'd want to go sailing or riding.'

'I'd just like one who was really good-looking, and nice and sent me flowers ...' Alison had started to say romantically, and then felt that the conversation was drifting off from the things that needed to be discussed. 'Look, I haven't finished explaining about the kitchen rota yet. Of course, it needn't concern you very much, as you're not living here, but you won't mind helping to clear away sometimes at lunch-time? Twice a week perhaps? I've worked out a sort of team system. Oh, and these are rough timetables that tell us what lessons are happening on various days of the week. We're all going skating tomorrow, assuming the pond's still frozen. And there's something about science lessons that's all going to be sorted out next week, apparently.'

Before Aunt Win came back there was a telephone call, which Mrs Drummond answered and then came up to tell them all about it. 'That was your auntie,' she told Geraldine, who opened the door to her knock. 'Very flustered, she was. Told me there'd be two extra to lunch. Apparently it isn't two girls who are coming to join us from Switzerland, but four! Could I have a couple of extra pairs of hands to help me get another bedroom ready? And who are today's volunteers for helping with laying the table and doing the lunch?'

There was a fluster of activity which, together with some time given to copying out the Shakespeare, kept them busy for the rest of the morning. Just as the clock struck one, Aunt Win was heard at the front door. There was a chatter of voices exclaiming over the cold, explaining about the extra girls, making welcoming noises, and the six girls upstairs ran down to join the gathering in the hall.

'Here we all are.' Aunt Win's voice had a note of slightly false jollity about it. 'Two more girls than we expected. Isn't that nice? It seems there was a mix-up, due to a misunderstanding. Here are Marie and Evangeline, from Switzerland, and this is Bernadette from France, who has been taking lessons with Evangeline for the past year, and Gabriele from Austria, who was my pupil two years ago and is keen to join us here at Four Winds.'

Everyone once again shook hands – this slightly formal greeting to each new arrival had now become a tradition at Four Winds – and then Aunt Win started ushering the new arrivals upstairs to be shown their rooms.

'Can I help, Aunt Win?' asked Geraldine, struggling to assist with Bernadette's suitcase.

'No, eet's OK, Madame Ontween, I too can do eet,' said Bernadette eagerly.

Jeannie started to giggle at this absurd version of Aunt Win's name and then realised that this was going to solve the problem of what everyone was to call her, because the Austrian girl, Gabriele, suddenly used it too, evidently thinking that this was the correct thing to do. 'Mrs Ontvinn, let me to help wiz der luggage,' she said politely, taking her cue from Bernadette.

'Just follow me up the stairs,' said Aunt Win smoothly, taking one of the cases with her. 'Help each other girls. Mrs Drummond, what extra room did you make ready?'

'Just follow Mrs Ontwin,' said Amanda carefully, to Marie and Evangeline, wondering how much English they understood. 'And lunch is nearly ready, too,' she added. 'You must be hungry.'

'Is Madame Ontveen zee correct name of zees lady?' asked Marie in a low voice to Amanda. 'I was told eet was Madame Bootle.'

'Well ...' Amanda was about to explain but Alison seized the moment. 'Yes, her name is Mrs Ontwin,' she announced. 'That's now been decided. In fact, you new girls have just solved a problem for us!'

And over lunch, amid some laughter, it was agreed that from now on, the headmistress of Four Winds was to be known as 'Mrs Ontwin' to everyone.

It was surprising how quickly the name caught on. Even Mr and Mrs Drummond started to use it. The only person who continued to call Aunt Win by her real name was Uncle Harry who, incidentally, soon became known as 'Major Ontwin' to everyone else. It was another part of what was rapidly becoming a special set of traditions, peculiar to Four Winds.

Chapter 5

That afternoon there was a good deal of administration to sort out. The four new girls had been allocated bedrooms, two to each room. To ensure each girl some privacy, Mr Drummond had brought up some folding screens that had been used to section off parts of the dining-room for dancing in the old hotel days. These meant that, although they had the companionship of shared bedrooms, every girl had her own space. Over the weeks they would put up pictures and posters, small ornaments and knick-knacks from home, making the place attractive and personal.

Telephone calls and faxes sorted out the confusion over the extra pupils from Switzerland. Aunt Win – sorry, Mrs Ontwin – had been more successful as a teacher than she had realised. Quickly, the word had spread among her former pupils in Switzerland and in Austria that she was now taking pupils at her own school in England. The four girls that arrived seemed likely to be followed by two or three more, if these sent back happy and enthusiastic reports. Poor Mrs Ontwin began to feel slightly overwhelmed. Should she spread the word that her little school was now full? On the other hand, there was still plenty of room at Four Winds, and no teacher likes to turn away pupils.

She began to feel the need, however, for some administrative support. There was no one to help her with office work. She had arranged for fees to be paid by the parents of the various girls, and all this would mean letters and a filing system. She had contacted the education authorities to ensure that they knew that the regulations concerning her pupils' schooling were being followed, that each girl was being given an education suited to her age and ability. As she had specialised in home-schooling pupils of different ages for some years, she knew all about the practicalities of the law and the importance of ensuring that its regulations were fulfilled.

It was clearly going to be impossible to run Four Winds without a secretary. And what about a matron to supervise the girls' welfare? At present there were only her and Mrs Drummond. Suppose one of the girls should fall ill or be dreadfully homesick? How could she look after them all, while teaching at the same time and sorting out an increasingly complicated timetable?

'One thing at a time,' she told herself steadily, as she went to supervise the afternoon's timetable.

Three of her new pupils spoke reasonable English – Marie, Gabriele, and Bernadette. Evangeline spoke a little but had forgotten much of it. Her languages were German and French. During lunch, Aunt Win had been kept busy translating for her. She decided to institute a new rule: one meal a week would be French-speaking only and one German-speaking. That would get the English girls hurrying to learn the languages! Of course the normal language of all lessons and activities would be English. Evangeline had been sent to England to learn the language and would soon pick it up. But it was essential that the other girls improve their languages too. This would be a school in which three languages would be spoken, as far as possible, by all the pupils.

She announced this, along with various other administrative matters, before starting the afternoon's lessons.

'Let's make Tuesday lunchtime our French meal,' she said, 'That gives us a full day to prepare, so you English girls can think up one or two full French sentences to say for lunch tomorrow! Then Friday lunchtime will be our German meal.' She repeated all this in both French and German so that all her pupils understood. Then the kitchen duties rota had to be explained in all three languages. Finally, it was time for the new arrivals to be shown round. Alison was given the task of doing this while the Brown twins, Amanda, Elizabeth and

Joan had a French lesson. Elizabeth was badly behind in French, as in various other subjects, and would have to share certain lessons with the younger girls.

After this, the music teacher arrived – more handshakes and greetings all round – and Alison went off with her to the music room which had been established, with the grand piano in it, next door to the schoolroom. While Aunt Win gave an English lesson to Evangeline, and the other girls worked quietly on various tasks – Geraldine, Jeannie, Amanda and Joan were learning their Shakespeare lines from the morning – the faint sounds of music came from next door. Alison was obviously a talented player. The music made a pleasant background to the afternoon's work. Everyone was rather sorry when it ended.

Much giggling accompanied the efforts in the kitchen to help Mrs Drummond with afternoon tea. Gabriele and Bernadette had joined with Geraldine to make up the team of helpers, and Gabriele splashed some milk on her skirt. Struggling with her English, she tried to ask if there wasn't a pinafore for her to wear. Once they grasped what she was trying to say, the idea seemed a good one, and searching in the cupboards, Geraldine found a pile of aprons, clearly designed for the hotel staff. They were crisp, white pinafores of the old-fashioned kind, with wide straps that went over the shoulders, crossed over, and buttoned on to the waist-band, which tied in a wide sash. The girls couldn't resist trying them on. Of course, being designed for grown-ups, they reached the floor on schoolgirls, the effect was hilarious but rather charming. Giggling madly, and thoroughly enjoying themselves, they brought up the tea-trays. They knew they'd create an effect when they entered the schoolroom, and were not disappointed.

'Oh, girls, wherever did you find them? You look like something out of a Victorian novel!' Aunt Win threw back her head in laughter.

'Hey, I want one! They're terrific!'

'Turn round. Try curtseying! You look sweet. Couldn't you find a mob-cap too?'

Everyone enjoyed the tea and scones, and afterwards there was a general scramble down to the kitchen where Alison led the search for more pinafores. Only Elizabeth stood aloof. 'It's all so childish,' she said sneeringly to Aunt Win. 'Who wants to play dressing-up games?'

'Oh, I don't know, it's fun discovering all the things in this old house,' said Aunt Win. 'And we certainly do need to have you girls in aprons for kitchen work. I wonder I hadn't thought of it before. I think you might find some more pinafores, girls, in the big linen cupboard on the top landing, so you might find it useful to rummage there. But don't get it all untidy and messed up.'

In the main linen cupboard there was a further stack of crisp pinafores, alongside beautiful table-cloths and damask napkins for dinner parties and ordinary things like towels, sheets and drying-up cloths. The cupboard was warm as it was heated by the pipes that brought hot water to the kitchen and bathrooms. It was a cosy cave full of fresh-smelling linen. When the girls returned, bearing armfuls of starched white cotton, Aunt Win enjoyed the general scrim-mage of trying-on and laughing, and then called a halt. 'Let's get this organised,' she said. 'Everyone can choose a pinny and after that can keep it, but you must put your name on it and then wear it for doing kitchen duty or other tasks. And though you do look hilarious with them reaching to the ground, we really must make them fit you properly. This evening we'll get out my sewing-machine, and you can all get needles and thread, and we'll take the hems up.'

In fact, nothing could have been better for breaking the ice that first evening with all the new girls than the pinning and stitching and laughing that went on with the fitting of the aprons. Joan and Elizabeth left after tea, Joan bearing hers so that her mother could help her adjust it to fit. Elizabeth had of course refused one, but was secretly beginning to regret it.

'Well, what did you think of our first day?' asked Joan as they trudged down the drive in the snow.

'It's lunatic,' said Elizabeth. 'We'll never learn anything. A lot of crazy foreign girls who can't speak English, and Mrs Ontwin or whatever her name is making us read Shakespeare. The only thing that was worthwhile was the food!'

'You did promise Mum you'd stick it out for a week,' Joan reminded her.

'I'm only doing it because we're marooned here in the snow,' her sister retorted. 'This time next week, or whenever it thaws, I'll be back at school and having a good laugh about all of this with all my friends, I can tell you.'

That evening, back at Four Winds, Uncle Harry – Major Ontwin – was brought in to enjoy the sight of the school in pinafores, while Mrs Drummond whirred away at a sewing-machine. Fluent in German, French and Italian, he had no difficulty in speaking to all the newly-arrived pupils. His style of bluff and cheerful courtesy made it impossible to be shy with him.

'This whole project's mad, of course,' he remarked cheer-ily to his wife as they made their way downstairs, leaving the girls clearing up before supper. 'Here we are, in this great house, with you supervising a great crowd of young ladies, and me planning a trip to Africa. Still, it makes for an interest-ing life doesn't it?' He did insist, however, that she get some more staff as a top priority. The number of pupils now made it possible to accept that the establishment was definitely a school, and it was essential to have someone sharing the burden of caring for the girls.

'I can't go away and leave you in sole charge,' he said. 'It'll all get ridiculous. Tomorrow, we'll find you some secretarial help and someone to act as matron.'

That night at supper, it again became apparent that some order and structure was needed. It was no use hoping people would just stroll into the dining-room on time. A bell had to be rung, and from now on this bell for meals meant that everyone had to obey its summons promptly. Aunt Win also noticed that Gabriele and Evangeline hesitated for a moment before taking up their spoons to start the soup, as if they expected something.

'You're quite right,' she said, 'we are not pagans. We'll say Grace before we eat, and we'll do that at lunch and supper every day. Harry, dear, would you like to say Grace tonight? And during the coming weeks we'll learn a French and a German version so we can vary it.'

Major Ontwin obliged by saying a dignified Grace in Latin, which impressed everyone. (It was the Grace used at his Cambridge college, which he had memorised from his university days.) The meal was a relaxed and happy one. Looking anxiously round the table, Aunt Win saw cheerful faces. She chatted in French to Evangeline, translating what others were saying. The food was good. Geraldine and Jeannie talked about the fax they were sending to Japan that evening, telling all their news. They'd even drawn pictures of themselves in pinafores.

Alison told Gabriele with obvious enthusiasm about her music lesson. Marie and Bernadette asked Amanda about the next day's activities and she told them – partly with signs and gestures – that they'd be going skating if the cold weather still held.

Much later, the headmistress made the rounds of the rooms after the girls were all in bed. She had quiet word with each of her pupils. Had they cleaned their teeth? Said their prayers? The rooms were cosy and the thick curtains shut out the snowy scene beyond. Tomorrow there'd be skating.

'It's much, much more fun than we even imagined, isn't it?' whispered Jeannie to Geraldine as they lay snuggled with hot water bottles in the room they shared with Amanda. 'Who'd be back at our old school, where the same thing seemed to happen day after day?'

'The odd thing here,' came Amanda's voice, also whispering, in the dark from the bed by the window, 'is that we're making it all up as we go along. I mean, today we just sort of invented another bit of uniform, along with the red hats. Pinafores for kitchen work. I wonder what comes next?'

Chapter 6

It was remarkable how quickly things developed into a school routine at Four Winds. The next day Elizabeth and Joan arrived with their mother, Mrs Hurry, who was to teach geography. She was well-equipped with an overhead projector and started the lesson with pictures and maps of Europe, before homing in on the countries that were represented in the schoolroom – Switzerland, Austria, France and Britain. With vivid illustrations, and with many questions to her listeners, she brought out the relevant features of each country and got everyone fascinated in an unforgettable lesson that made them hungry for more. Leaving them with quite a lot of homework, and a keen feeling that geography was going to be one of their favourite subjects for the term ahead, she then swept off to a well-deserved coffee-break, before settling down to help Aunt Win with some badly-needed office work.

The afternoon saw everyone down at the village pond, skating. Jeannie was in her element here. She adored skating and this was the first time she had ever done it in the open air.

'It's quite different from being at a rink!' she squeaked in excitement, the first to venture on the ice, which had been carefully checked by experts sent in by the local authorities, and pronounced safe. 'Come on! It's fabulous!' Evangeline was the next to join her on the ice, and the two crossed hands and skated along together, wobbling a bit and swerving suddenly to avoid others, but on the whole presenting an impressive picture. The other girls were of mixed ability.

Both Joan and Elizabeth had skated at the local rink, but not for some while, and Amanda and Alison were newcomers to the sport. Gabriele proved a competent skater and urged on Marie and Bernadette.

The crisp, cold air tingled against the girls' faces as they skated, and whisked away any sense of stuffiness from a morning spent indoors. Their cries of laughter rang out in the frosty air, and the skates made a satisfying slicing sound as they cut and curved across the ice.

Aunt Win cheered from the sidelines. She was glad to get out of the house and away from the paperwork and burdens of being a headmistress. The work was beginning to tell on her. She looked and felt tired. And this was only the beginning!

Back at the house, the kitchen team for the day changed eagerly into pinafores. Without anyone saying so, it had become a definite rule that these were to be worn for all household tasks. Tea was a popular meal and was followed by a further lesson period before another break before supper. Then the day-girls would normally have gone home, but tonight they stayed on because their mother was to be in charge for the evening, giving the headmistress a chance to relax. There was a time of kitchen-work and general tidying-up and then the evening meal, after which there would be homework and then some free time.

Taking advantage of Mrs Hurry's being with them for the day, Aunt Win and Uncle Harry had their supper privately together in their own room.

'Goodness, it's nice just to be the two of us!' said Aunt Win, kicking off her shoes. 'We've only got a couple of weeks or so before you go away, and I feel I'm neglecting you.'

'Not a bit of it,' said her husband cheerily, enjoying his meal and giving his wife an affectionate grin. 'Frankly, I see this whole school venture as a sort of extended joke, and so long as you are not too tired, I think it's all great fun. This is a beautiful house and will be a marvellous place in the spring and summer, but we couldn't possibly live in it all by ourselves and I certainly have no desire to run an hotel. Just at the moment, this school idea seems to suit us all admirably.'

'But all the same, I'd like to take a run up to town as soon as the thaw comes,' admitted Aunt Win thoughtfully. 'I'd like to see that all's well at the London flat, bring down one or two more of our favourite bits and pieces, and possibly think about getting in some short-term tenants for the next couple of months. It would bring in some useful money and I don't like to think of the place being empty.'

'I've already been working on that,' said her husband, putting down his knife and fork and reaching over for some papers. 'I contacted a couple of people to see if they knew of anyone who'd need a flat on a short-term basis and Roderick faxed me this from Japan. It's a chap from his firm who's coming to London to deal with a contract that will all be over by Easter. Sounds ideal to me. What do you think?'

Comfortably, husband and wife talked through their domestic arrangements, enjoying Mrs Drummond's excellent coffee and some of their favourite music while they relaxed together.

Over in the school dining room, things were rather different. There seemed so much to discuss and in so many different languages! The skating had given everyone some badly-needed fresh air. There were plans to go again tomorrow. People were still giggling over pinafores, and this had raised the general question of school clothing. The new girls had discovered, when the group trooped out to walk down to the pond, that the four original pupils had decked themselves out in matching red berets and scarves, and they wanted to know why they hadn't been informed that this was the school uniform.

'Well, it wasn't an official uniform originally,' said Amanda, trying to explain. 'It just sort of happened.'

'On a railway station,' added Geraldine helpfully.

'We thought it would make it easier for Mrs Ontwin to recognise us, and we enjoyed the fun of all being dressed alike,' said Alison. 'There's absolutely no reason why you shouldn't join in, of course.'

Evangeline, who had been baffled by much of the conversation, slowly understood it as parts of it were translated to her by a confusing array of voices. She talked earnestly in French to Bernadette.

43

'She say – we all say,' said Bernadette, nodding round at the other new girls, on whose behalf she was now speaking, 'we too want red hats. Please we go tomorrow and buy?'

'I don't see why not,' said Mrs Hurry. 'I'm sure it could be arranged. Why don't we see if Major Ontwin or Mr Drummond could drive some of you on a shopping trip some time over the next few days?'

While she spoke enthusiastically, however, she was acutely conscious of her own two daughters, both pupils alongside these others but conspicuously less keen on wearing any kind of uniform. Of course it was rather different being day-girls. And the uniform might be a novelty for foreigners but was something quite ordinary and tedious for British school-girls. In fact, one argument that she had used in getting Elizabeth to Four Winds in the first place was that she would-n't have to wear one. There was an awkward silence as the subject of the hats died away. The girls on kitchen-duty helped to stack and carry the plates. Everyone enjoyed using the hatch down to the kitchen with its fascinating system of pulleys. Some delicious puddings now appeared and people served themselves with lemon meringue or trifle according to taste. The conversation moved on to other subjects.

A new teacher was to make her appearance the next day – Miss Crisp, who was to teach maths. She was also to be in charge of science, but how could this be taught without a science laboratory? No one knew, although Mrs Hurry was aware that Aunt Win was in the process of opening negotia-tions with a nearby boys' junior school which had an excellent lab which they might be prepared to rent out to the Four Winds girls on one evening a week. It would be inconve-nient to drive girls over there for lessons but it might just work as a temporary arrangement.

After supper and clearing-up, Mrs Hurry and her girls left and the others made themselves comfortable in their own sitting-room. A television had now been installed, but after switching around the various channels the girls found nothing that they specially wanted to see. The video machine was still downstairs, awaiting installation. Bernadette went off to get some sewing to do. Someone asked Alison what she was reading.

'It's *The Prisoner of Zenda*,' she said. 'I've just started it. Apparently it's quite a famous book, and all about an Englishman who gets mistaken for the king of a foreign country and falls in love with a princess.'

'Don't keep it to yourself, then,' urged Amanda. 'Start reading it aloud.'

At first Alison wouldn't, but bribed with chocolates by the others ('You won't get any unless you do!') she began the story in her clear and pleasant voice. The girls sat in the deep comfortable armchairs and looked at the flickering fire, munched chocolates and became lost in the tale.

Bed times had by now been clearly established and were announced by a bell. Aunt Win carefully patrolled every bedroom before she herself retired for the night. She made sure that all the curtains were drawn against the bitter cold, whispered goodnight to anyone still awake, and assured herself that no one was crying or ill or unhappy.

For the next few days the freezing weather continued. Every day there was skating on the pond. The enterprising owner of the skating-rink in the nearby town had established a makeshift stand from which he hired out skates, and pretty soon he was joined by a cafe-owner who started selling coffee and hot mulled wine. At Four Winds the new maths mistress made her appearance and was young, cheerful, competent and popular. The arrangement for using the prep school science laboratory went ahead, and the first batch of pupils went over there for an evening lesson.

Gradually, the school developed a sense of structure and routine. At first they had all sat round one big table and relied on the chiming of a clock to remind them that an hour or half-hour had passed and that a changeover of lessons was due. Now they spread into two groups or even three, with language classes being held in a neighbouring room, piano lessons in the music-room, cookery downstairs and a sewing-class beginning one afternoon cosily round the fireplace in the hall. So a bell system was introduced with Mr Drummond, or one of the girls appointed for the duty if he was busy elsewhere, pressing a buzzer which echoed on the old hotel public-address system throughout the building.

Uncle Harry took orders for red hats and scarves and gave

himself an hilarious trip into town to buy them, distributing them in the evening amid much laughter and trying-on and posing in front of mirrors. Still nothing was said about the two Hurry girls, and everyone quietly felt that the uniform question was heading for some form of confrontation.

Aunt Win made plans for a London visit, with lists of things she needed to buy and people she needed to see. She had to register Four Winds with the educational authorities, she wanted to make sure the school was properly covered for fire inspections, and she needed to visit the official examination authorities to check about the correct syllabus material. Some new text-books were on order but there were some videos that might be worth renting from a library for a history project. She had also decided that the girls needed an outing to see a couple of Shakespeare plays. It was no use just reading him; you had to see it acted.

With more teachers now part of the team, Aunt Win and Uncle Harry were able to have more time to themselves and to enjoy their evening meals alone together. The cookery classes proved popular and successful, and everyone enjoyed eating the results.

Every night saw Alison reading aloud to those girls who were interested, while the others chattered in one language or another, tried the television (the reception was rather poor in this particular area so they tended not to bother with it) or taught each other games. 'Monopoly' became a sudden craze, initiated by Uncle Harry who challenged his nieces to a game one evening and then found himself teaching the game to interested foreigners.

It might have been expected that the girls would divide into two groups – the original four and then the 'foreign new girls' – but it didn't work out like that. English Alison struck up a strong friendship with the Austrian Gabriele who was closer to her in age than the other girls. They discovered a shared passion for riding and swapped books and pictures of horses and ponies. Gabriele had brought a beautiful little group of china ponies which she stood on her bedside table. Both girls pored over the book that Alison had been given for Christmas. There were riding stables not far from Four Winds: Gabriele's parents were keen for her to go riding

46

regularly and had specifically requested this when making school arrangements with Aunt Win. 'My father owns a big stables not far from Vienna,' explained Gabriele. 'I adore horses. I grew up with them. England is famous for its riding. I can't wait to explore some of the local countryside and to have a gallop over these hills.'

'I need to work on a lot of basic riding skills,' said Alison. 'I get some riding in the holidays at a local stables but I've never had a pony of my own. It would be an absolute dream to be able to go riding from here. I'm going to ask my parents about it.'

'One day you must come to Austria and see our stables,' said Gabriele eagerly. 'Look, here are some snaps of them.'

Meanwhile, the younger girls were forging links too. The twins and Amanda naturally made a team but increasingly Bernadette was part of it, while Marie and Evangeline had become close friends. Joan Hurry had become friendly with Evangeline too. Aunt Win had specifically asked her to help the girl with her English and the two always took their coffee – and tea-breaks together, often dissolving into giggles over their attempts to understand one another but always having fun and enjoying one another's company. Only Elizabeth Hurry stood aloof. She didn't share Alison's and Gabriele's interest in horses and was understandably bored by the company of the younger girls. Aunt Win felt uncomfortable that Elizabeth was obviously cross and unhappy about coming to Four Winds, and was already putting her mind to ways of dealing with this. She found herself thinking that one helpful addition would be a couple more older pupils but she hurriedly corrected herself. She had never intended to run a full-scale school. Every pupil that arrived was essentially taking part in an experiment. It wasn't something that should be allowed to grow out of hand.

The boarders kept in touch with their families through letters and faxes and shared news that came back from them. It was an exciting moment when a fax arrived on Aunt Win's fax machine downstairs in her study, or when the postman arrived with letters with overseas stamps on them. Jeannie and Geraldine got faxes from their parents, full of descriptions of Japan and loving affectionate family messages. By post there also came a packet of drawings from their little brothers. The Continental girls got long letters in German or in French. Aunt Win instituted a system for people to send faxes or use the telephone at a set time in the evening. She made it a rule that everyone must write home at least once a week, but most were keen to do this anyway.

And then the thaw came. Just ten days after their first skating session it suddenly seemed warmer; the bitter cutting edge of the wind had subsided. A faint dripping noise was heard as the trees started to shed their snow, and by mid-afternoon great chunks of snow were sliding off the roof and crashing with a satisfying noise on to the lawn below. There would be no more skating. Two days later the garden emerged as brown and mushy and wet, with benches and a sundial and flower-beds revealed without their blanket of snow.

The first thing the thaw brought was Grandma. She drove all the way from her small cottage, enthusiastic to see this new school which had been established by members of her own family. Geraldine and Jeannie excitedly dragged her round every part of the building, showing her their bedroom, their own special places in the schoolroom and their latest efforts at learning the piano. They paraded in their pinafores and the other girls came hurrying over to show theirs, too. She had a long talk with Aunt Win and it was decided that she would visit again, this time to stay the night and give Win and Harry the chance of a trip to London. She took photographs of her granddaughters to send to their parents in Japan, gave them warm hugs and packets of home-made fudge, and went home to write a long and enthusiastic letter all about Four Winds.

The thaw brought other visitors. The first was Father Higgins and Canis. They both now knew the girls well from their regular Sunday visits to church and were given a friendly welcome. It was during the mid-morning break, and the girls were having hot chocolate round the hall fire. Amanda was on duty for errands and ran to open the door. Priest and dog bounded into the house with enthusiasm and Father Higgins was soon chatting to everyone while Canis explored the hall and ran excitedly round with discoveries like wellington boots and spare pinafores.

'I really came to see your headmistress,' Father Higgins said, calling Canis firmly to order. 'Is she in her office?'

'Yes, I've told her you're here. She's on the telephone but said we were to give you some coffee or chocolate and she'd be with you as soon as she could,' said Amanda. 'It's been a busy morning. We had a history lesson and then English Literature, and so she's only just managed to get into her office to deal with phone messages and letters and things.'

While they waited for her to finish the phone call, they told him the latest school news: about plans for riding lessons at a local stables, about the huge snowman they had all made on the front lawn which was still standing while all the rest of the snow had disappeared, and about the tradition which had developed of singing all the way on journeys in the school van to science lessons at Medthorpe Manor boys' school on Wednesday evenings. 'We have to stop once we arrive there because they all think we're mad anyway,' said Alison. 'The little boys are all at supper while we're having our lesson but we sometimes see them in the corridor as we finish, and they always pull faces at us or make signs behind our backs. The science lab is a good one and it's only used by the biggest boys. Some of them have carved their names on the benches.'

'And left chewing-gum on the underside of the seats,' added Gabriele, wrinkling up her nose.

'And toffee papers on the floor,' said Bernadette. 'But they are nice little boys,' she added, 'I feel sorry for them, being at school and away from their parents. Several come from Africa and Japan and even Russia, all to get an English education.'

They were all enjoying sitting and talking, but fairly quickly Aunt Win came out, apologising for keeping Father Higgins waiting. Once settled in her office he came straight to the point.

'As I mentioned a while ago, my sister Tessa and her husband are coming to stay, bringing their little girl, Amy. She's been unwell and away from school for quite a while. They feel a change would do her good. They like this area and were thinking of buying a house here but were wondering about schools. Would you consider taking Amy? I think a small school with a friendly atmosphere would suit her.

49

Could I suggest that they all come and see you?'

Aunt Win laughed, 'Oh, send her along,' she said. 'I've given up trying to pretend I'm not really running a school. We're not actually registered as an educational establishment, you know. It's just a private arrangement. I'm essentially a teacher of languages – French, German, and English – and of history, and I've got people helping me out with other subjects. The girls who are boarding here call it a school. They're inventing traditions all the time and even a uniform of sorts, and I've divided them into classes or groups for their lessons, but essentially we all live together more or less as a family. Your little niece might find it all a bit overwhelming. How old is she?'

'She's not so small, really – twelve, I think, but because of her illness she seems rather young for her age. I think her parents would like the atmosphere here. Amy wouldn't board at first, of course, as they'll all be staying with me at St Mary's presbytery. But if it all worked out well and Amy was happy, perhaps she could become a boarder later on while they decided about where to live?'

'Of course. There's still plenty of room. Just suggest to them that they telephone and we'll fix a time for them to call. It's rather absurd the way I seem to be collecting pupils all the time! But to be honest, I'd rather prefer, if any more new arrivals come, that they are older girls. There are only three of the bigger girls here at present and that makes life a bit dull for them. And I'm having trouble finding some staff, too,' Aunt Win added as an afterthought. 'I haven't found anyone to teach Latin, and although the girls don't want to learn it, I'm determined that they shall! It's a vitally important part of a really well-rounded education, especially for anyone who wants a good grasp of modern European languages and of history. And then, quite separately, there's the problem of our domestic arrangements. The girls are splendid at helping out and doing lots of odd tasks but I can't really ask them to spend hours at their laundry or making sure the bathrooms are clean. It isn't fair on them and interrupts their education. I suppose what I really need is a matron to look after all that side of things.' Her voice tailed away and for a moment she was absorbed in this problem.

Father Higgins' voice brought her back to earth again. 'Well, as to Latin,' he said, 'as a temporary measure, I could teach that, if you like. I was actually a Classics teacher at a boys' school, you know, before I decided to give it all up to become a priest. I've never taught girls before but I'm willing to give it a try if it's only for, say, a couple of mornings a week.'

'Do you really mean it? I must say, I'd be terribly grateful. Just as a temporary thing, of course, until I can get something organised through a teaching agency.'

'Yes, of course. No, don't worry about payment, we'll discuss that later, once you've seen if I'm any good or not. I'll give you the number of the school where I worked so you can find out their opinion of me if you like. Goodness, is that the time? I must rush. Mrs McMurdoch, my housekeeper, always does a hot cooked lunch for me on Thursdays and gets annoyed if I'm not there to eat it. She's a kindly soul but can be a bit of a dragon when she wants. And before I get back, I've two other calls to make. No, don't worry about seeing me out. I'll leave you to your work. Come on, Canis!' And with his usual energy he bounded off, Canis alongside, both somehow looking rather alike as they bounced energetically down the drive.

Aunt Win felt much relieved after this conversation, and after looking at the timetable to see how the Latin classes could be fitted in, she turned to the stack of papers on her desk that needed attention. The buzzer had already gone, marking the end of the morning break, and the girls were upstairs having a maths or a music lesson. There was a pleasant air of purposeful bustle about the school. In spite of all the challenges and worries it was presenting, it was rather fun being headmistress at Four Winds!

But the thaw had brought to a head a problem that everyone had known was there: the question of Elizabeth and Joan Hurry's future at the school.

'I only ever said I'd give it a week, and I only agreed to go there because we simply couldn't get to a proper school because of the snow,' Elizabeth had argued angrily with her mother the first morning that the snow had finally gone and she no longer felt she needed to go to Four Winds.

51

'Oh come on, be reasonable, you can't back out now,' her mother pleaded. 'It's all beginning to go so well. Just give it a while longer. And Joan's happy there. You can see all your friends from your old school at weekends, you know, and I'll drive you into town to be with them if there's something special on.'

They arrived at school that morning late, with Joan in tears. Everyone sensed that something was badly wrong. Elizabeth was sullen and cross. It all finally exploded two days later in a row between her and Alison over, inevitably perhaps, the question of school uniforms.

Jeannie and Bernadette had found in a cupboard, while they were helping Mrs Drummond to tidy up, some bolts of grey-blue cloth that had apparently been ordered a year or two earlier to make uniforms for the hotel staff.

'Very smart they used to look,' Mrs Drummond said proudly. 'Nice little jackets and skirts. They used to get them made up in any design they wanted, by a tailor. The men had a different uniform, darker material. I don't think there's any of that here. It was heavier stuff for their suits. This blue-grey is a beautiful tweed. It doesn't seem right just to have it go to waste.'

'Oh, it won't go to waste, Mrs Drummond!' breathed Jeannie excitedly. 'We can have it for our school uniforms!'

And before Mrs Drummond could object, or indeed make any comment at all, she had passed on the idea via Bernadette and Geraldine and Marie, and soon it was over Four Winds that there was going to be a uniform, blue-grey skirts or tunics with bands of red velvet ribbon just above the hems. (The ribbon was Geraldine's idea, with the extra detail of velvet being a thoughtful addition by Alison.)

Enthusiasm ran high, and at lunch-time the details were being worked out. Aunt Win learned with surprise that Grandma, Mrs Drummond, and perhaps even Mrs Hurry, were going to be invited to get their sewing-machines whirring. There was some debate about whether or not people could wear their own shirts and jerseys with the new skirts, or whether obligatory red or white ones ought to be imposed.

'Here, just a minute! Calm down everyone,' cried Aunt

Win, feeling that she ought to get on top of this situation. 'I really can't have you all dictating to poor Mrs Drummond and others about a lot of extra sewing work. If you insist on having these uniforms you'll have to help with making them yourselves. And before you start getting all excited, let's make sure there really is agreement about this venture so that we can make a firm commitment and stick to it.'

There was a general babble of talk. Geraldine and Jeannie were firmly in favour of uniform, as were Amanda, Alison, Evangeline, Bernadette and Marie. Gabriele thought aloud about it.

'It is a good thing for some reasons,' she said. 'It would mean that we all dress alike and so no one is smarter or has better clothes than others. Also, it would mean we can keep our own clothes for the weekends, and this I like. How I explain? Well, already I am beginning to feel I did not bring enough with me. Somehow I feel I must look different every day, must show smart clothes all the time.'

The other girls nodded. Bernadette then chipped in with another reason for liking uniforms: 'Me, I like too the English tradition. Oh, and I want to send photograph to my parents that I am at school in England! They will smile and show to everyone!'

'Well, that's all right for you, but what about those of us who find the idea horrible?' cut in Elizabeth's voice suddenly and angrily. Everyone was jerked into sudden silence.

'You just imagine Joan and me, walking down through the village and wearing a uniform that no one locally has seen before except on the hotel staff,' Elizabeth went on. 'We'll feel and look stupid. It's just a silly game to all of you younger ones, and to you, Alison,' she added suddenly. 'You think the whole thing's like something out of a story. Red velvet ribbons! You always dress to look old-fashioned anyway. I suppose you think you're going to look like Princess Flavia in that silly book you're reading!'

'Elizabeth! Really, there's no need to be unpleasant.' Aunt Win's voice was sharp. 'I shall call an end to this discussion in a minute, if we can't all talk in a civilised way to one another. Now, Evangeline, you had something to say?'

'I sink,' Evangeline struggled with her English, 'Alison eez not so old-fashioned. But Elizabeth think Alison is because Alison only have small number of clothes here, and not able to make new every day as Elizabeth does. Same for us all.' This was essentially the same point that Gabriele had made, but there was something more, too. Evangeline came from a wealthy home and had brought quite a lot of luggage, including some very fashionable clothes with the latest designer labels. She was not particularly interested in showing off, and had already been a little embarrassed when some of the other girls had admired her shoes or jeans or talked about getting their own parents to buy similar ones for them. It would make things much easier if there was less fashion pressure.

Aunt Win was anxious to draw the discussion to a close but knew that it wasn't really over yet. 'Well,' she said, after some more discussion and argument had gone back and forth, 'we'll have a vote on it. No, not now, later on today, or better still, tomorrow. We'll have it tomorrow lunchtime. It can be a private ballot, a secret vote so that no one need feel under any pressure. I shall cut up some squares of paper and put boxes for you to tick 'yes' or 'no' for uniform. As to the uniform itself, yes, we'll use the material we have here, as it will save my having to write to all your parents asking them to spend money on more clothes. And if – and I mean if, because we haven't decided yet – we go ahead, we'll have some joint sewing-sessions and we can all help make them, using a simple design.'

She looked round to make sure everyone was listening. 'Now, remember, if you decide to say 'yes' it will become a rule for everyone; I shall insist that you all wear uniform on weekdays, at least during school hours. We'll decide what it is to be – and don't let's have any silly ideas but just something straightforward and wearable – and then you must all abide by it.'

There was plenty to discuss with all of this, and the talk about it went on at intervals all afternoon. Unfortunately, attitudes hardened. Elizabeth became more and more intransigent, saying that she thought not only the uniforms but a whole lot of ideas at Four Winds were silly. That, of course, angered most of the others and Alison in particular, at whom many of her remarks were addressed. Joan burst into tears because she didn't want to be disloyal to her sister but didn't want to be seen to agree with her. Gabriele announced firmly that she supported uniforms and thought that the three older ones in the school ought not to disagree violently but debate things in a calm way as an example to the rest, at which Bernadette, Amanda and the twins suddenly all at the same time got cross because they felt she was being patronising.

It was an awkward, rather silent and fractious group which gathered at teatime round the hall fire. The usual friendliness was gone, and Aunt Win and Miss Crisp both felt it acutely as they crossed the hall on their way from the study, where they had been battling with the computer which wouldn't work properly.

'I'm just so cross and fed up with the stupid thing,' Aunt Win was saying. 'It makes me despair. I could give up, I really could.'

Such was the mood of the girls sitting round the fire with their mugs of tea, that most of them assumed that Aunt Win was talking about uniforms. It was only when she went on to talk about 'That horrible machine – all the work I've been doing for the past hour has been lost and wasted' that they realised it was the computer that had brought on this fit of annoyance. Miss Crisp was cross too. As mathematics teacher she had felt that she somehow ought to know all about computers, but in fact she was not much use with this one and was frustrated by her own inability to solve its mysteries.

'We've been trying to print out some timetables for all of you,' she explained, warming her hands round her mug and standing before the fire, 'but the thing won't print properly, and at least part of what we had been doing has mysteriously disappeared from the screen. I'm prepared to admit defeat. But I don't like a machine getting the better of me!'

There was a general polite murmur of sympathy and then Elizabeth suddenly spoke up. 'I'm OK with computers,' she said. 'I've never been defeated by one yet. Let me go and look at it.'

Miss Crisp and Aunt Win looked at one another. Elizabeth was not their easiest pupil. She had shown no real interest in any lessons, was as rude as she dared to be when any teacher showed any friendliness, and had repeatedly made it clear that she was only a temporary visitor at Four Winds and disliked being there. But none of this was reason not to be grateful for her help with the computer.

'Oh Elizabeth, yes, do. How wonderful!' said Aunt Win with real warmth in her voice. 'Let me show you what we've been doing. I'm sure we've been getting it all wrong. There's a handbook, but I can't make head or tail of it after the first chapter.'

She put down her mug and led the way back to her office. There, making a mysterious humming noise and looking rather pleased with itself, was the computer that had been causing her such annoyance. With studied casualness, Elizabeth sat down in the swivel chair and looked at the keyboard. She pressed a letter experimentally.

'Mmm, I think I can handle this,' she said, staring at the screen. 'What did you name the file?' After a few more technical questions, she seemed to be in charge. After a while, Aunt Win tiptoed out. Presently the buzzer went, indicating that a fresh lesson was to start, but Elizabeth did not reappear from the study. She was due to join Alison and Gabriele for some French conversation but they started without her. No one liked to comment on her absence. At one point, leaving the two girls copying out some new words and phrases, Aunt Win went tentatively downstairs. Elizabeth did not even notice her as she peered round the study door. Her face a study in dedication, she was busy with the computer. Already half a dozen perfectly printed timetables lay on the desk beside her and she was now busy with another on the screen, making some minor adjustments.

'Did you want this version, labelled Group Three?' she asked, without bothering to greet her headmistress or make any comment about having missed the lesson. 'I've slightly shortened it by turning the word "mathematics" to "maths" to make it fit the page. There! That looks better. Now I'll print it off.'

She spoke with quiet authority and evident confidence, a completely different girl from the sullen one usually seen round the table at lessons.

'Yes ... oh, that looks super,' said Aunt Win gratefully. She hardly dared sound too enthusiastic. 'It's marvellous. You're terrific Elizabeth.'

'Oh, it's not that complicated really.' Elizabeth's face looked in danger of reverting to its usual sullen look. Aunt Win, speaking very low so as not to entice a change of mood, repeated her thanks.

'I suppose you wouldn't feel able to print off a couple of letters for me?' she asked humbly. 'I feel sure they are trapped in this machine too. I wrote something yesterday that wouldn't print off properly and eventually I just left it. I haven't had a chance to work on it today.'

'Of course.' Elizabeth was evidently enjoying her new-found confidence. 'What's the file-name?'

They both bent together over the computer, while Aunt Win pointed out the items that needed attention. There were two or three other letters that could be amended and printed off too. It was a quarter of an hour later that she finally remembered the two girls waiting upstairs. 'I'd better go now,' she said. 'Can you come up and join us in a bit? Or would you like to wait downstairs when you've finished?'

'I'll wait here,' said Elizabeth. 'It'll take me a moment or two to deal with this. How many copies do you want of each letter? Is there a photocopier I could use?'

'Over here.' Aunt Win showed her how it operated. 'It means a lot being able to trust you with letters,' she said. 'As you can see, these are about ordering some geography books, and insurance matters to do with the car. It's all quite important for the school.'

Elizabeth made a vague polite noise of acquiescence. Later, when the French lesson was over and she and Joan were ready to go home, Aunt Win took her aside for a further private word of thanks. Without saying so, they both felt that a new sort of solidarity had been established. That evening Mrs Hurry, who had been expecting a further outburst about the silliness of Four Winds, was agreeably surprised at supper to discover that Elizabeth instead talked about computing, waxing enthusiastically about Four Winds' latest equipment. 'That hotel really had all the latest technology,' she said. 'They must have designed their own brochures and everything. There's superb artwork and a fantastic spell-check facility that works really fast and doesn't waste time.'

The next day at school Aunt Win made a point of making a polite reference to the assistance Elizabeth had given with letters, quietly showing that she considered her to have shown a certain trustworthiness. As if picking up her mood, Alison deliberately deferred to her judgement over one or two small matters that cropped up during the morning – amendments to the kitchen-help rota where Elizabeth's commonsense suggestion sorted out a minor problem – and Gabriele deliberately asked her advice about their home-work.

It was due to be a German-speaking lunch. They had stuck to the rule that Aunt Win had decreed, of having one French and one German meal during the week. So far, no one had been a spoiler and deliberately refused to take part. There were some long silences from the English girls but each had deliberately learned one or two sentences and rather enjoyed struggling to make conversation or even to crack jokes in a foreign tongue.

But first came the vote on uniform. Surprisingly, Elizabeth herself volunteered to print out the ballot-forms, and when these were distributed everyone voted quickly and silently, putting the papers into a box placed by Aunt Win's study for the purpose. Father Higgins had come that morning to make arrangements about Latin lessons and it was unanimously agreed that he should do the counting. He took the matter seriously and carefully counted the total number of ballot papers to make sure everyone had voted, before unfolding each one in a private corner.

'It's a one hundred per cent decision,' he announced at the end. 'Everyone has voted for uniform. One ballot paper has "provided it's nothing too daft" written on it, and I must say I'm inclined to agree with that. As I don't know any of your handwriting, I don't know who wrote it, but I think it's sound advice!'

Of course, everyone suspected Elizabeth but no one could talk about it as at that moment the bell went for lunch, and all remarks had to be in German. This turned out to be more fun than usual, as Father Higgins joined them for the meal, gamely speaking what German he knew in an atrocious accent that had them all laughing. Then they all went out of doors to get some fresh air. It was again bitterly cold, but there was no snow. He started an impromptu game of rounders with a piece of wood and someone remembered finding a real rounders bat in the hall cupboard and ran to fetch it. The debate about uniforms was forgotten as gradually everyone joined in the game. When they reassembled, glowing and cheerful, for afternoon lessons the matter somehow seemed already settled. The next day, cutting and sewing began. Elizabeth, having decided to join in with the uniform idea, turned out to be quite enthusiastic.

Aunt Win and Mrs Hurry had between them chosen a simple pinafore-dress design. The blue-grey material was beautifully easy to sew and the results were charming. Red or cream blouses, bought locally, were also part of the outfit, and each girl needed several so as to have a fresh one each day. Grandma drove over again to help with the sewing. It was fun to watch the sewing-machine whirring, or to sit companionably stitching at hems round the fireplace, with some music in the background from Joan's tape recorder which she'd brought up to school for the purpose. Even the double bands of red velvet, two inches above the hem of each skirt, were universally agreed to look very attractive. Within a few days the pupils of Four Winds School were in matching grey-blue outfits.

Chapter 7

Father Higgins' Latin lessons, which many of the girls had been dreading because they thought the subject would be boring and difficult, turned out to be tremendous fun. He made the language interesting by showing how it could be used to say quite normal things, and by the end of the very first lesson the girls were greeting each other with 'Salve' and asking what was for lunch and what games would be played that afternoon, albeit in a halting way and with much use of the cheerful illustrated textbooks which he had brought with him. These he had obtained in a bookshop in town and were of an up-to-date modern design, showing people having ordinary conversations in Latin, with silly captions and lots of jokes. The lesson proved hilarious. It even produced the idea (from Bernadette) that they might have a Latin lunch each week, to add to the French and German ones already on the timetable.

'Oh no!' groaned Amanda. 'That's too much! That would only leave two lunches a week where we could talk English!'

'And all the breakfasts and suppers!' Gabriele reminded her. 'Remember that for some of us the French and German meals truly are a relief. It is a joy to be able to speak our own tongues.' And she grinned as she added, 'Also to have French and Austrian food,' for this had been a recent addition to the scheme. Mrs Drummond had decided to blend the cookery lessons with the theme of the lunches, and so now they had German bratwurst or Austrian sachertorte on the German-speaking days, and French casseroles or tasty omelettes on the French days. Cookery books with regional recipes were being studied so menus could be expanded and new ideas tried all the time.

'We'll have to invite Father Higgins to the Latin lunch if it's going to work properly,' said Jeannie. 'None of us can speak it properly, not even Aunt Win, and there are going to be long silences if there's no one to help out.'

'What about your dragon housekeeper, Father?' asked Geraldine. 'Would she let you come?'

Mrs McMurdoch, whom none of the girls had actually met, was becoming a famous figure in the school. Father Higgins was evidently slightly scared of her.

'The trouble is that she just doesn't have enough to do,' he explained. 'She has her own small house in the village and she bustles over every day to the presbytery. She wants to be helpful to the Church but there is very little that needs doing. A team of people clean the church regularly and the house is small with only me in it. I don't eat much breakfast, have a sandwich at lunchtime and can easily cook myself a meal in the evenings. During the day I am out most of the time: there's the hospital in Medchester to visit and I'm chaplain at the prison too. There are several sick people who are confined to their homes whom I visit regularly. On Tuesday and Thursday evenings I have Confirmation classes, and there are meetings with people who are getting married or having their children baptised. So it's rather a nuisance to have Mrs McMurdoch, who really is a very good soul, hoovering and bustling around.'

He was sorting exercise books busily as he spoke, and stopped to give Canis an affectionate pat. The room was bright and cheerful, with a cosy atmosphere. Everyone enjoyed these opportunities to chat to Father Higgins when the lesson had ended. Although he was a busy person he always had time for a few minutes of talk to round things off. He looked round at the cheerful faces of his pupils and sighed slightly as he thought of his rather fearsome housekeeper. 'She gave up her own job not long ago and I think she is regretting it. She likes to help people and I wish there was other work that could be found for her to do.'

'Does she really bully you about coming to meals on time?' asked Alison, sitting on the edge of a desk and rocking it satisfyingly as they talked. It was funny to think of Father Higgins, tall and energetic in his black cassock, a ferocious battler on the rounders pitch, teacher of Latin and well-known to everyone in the village, scurrying in fear of a bossy lady nagging him into his dining-room.

'It's ghastly,' said Father Higgins. 'Oh, she means well, but quite honestly it's rather intimidating. She hurries every-where and always seems to be making extra work! So on a busy morning, when I have to be off somewhere, she will remind me there's a steak-and-kidney pie to be eaten up for supper and ask me if it would be convenient for her to polish the bannisters or count the teaspoons or something. And she's the organiser of the team of ladies who clean the church, and they don't need organising. And she's started checking and listing all the towels and sheets in the house, just for something to do!'

'You've got to stand up to her,' said Geraldine. 'Have a campaign to assert your independence.'

'Well, there are other things to deal with,' said Father Higgins, putting on his coat. 'Today at any rate she's busy in her own small cottage. I've got my sermon to prepare for Sunday now, and confessions this evening, and tomorrow some other priests and I are having a day of prayer together to plan for Lent. Where's my scarf? Thanks. I really ought to get going. You've got that homework list clear, haven't you? I'll be seeing you next week – oh, and on Sunday, of course.'

'Don't let the dragon bite you!' called the twins cheekily as he and Canis, who always came to lessons, bounded down the stairs and out to his bicycle by the front door. The talk in the classroom turned to outdoor topics. Geraldine was keen to get more sports activities going. Four Winds had two tennis courts which could easily be used for netball, but they'd have to adapt the usual rules of the game to create smaller teams. At present the most popular game was rounders, again adapted for smaller numbers. Buying a netball and some posts would introduce a much-needed variety.

'There's a swimming-pool too,' Jeannie reminded her, 'round at the back, near the tennis courts.'

'But it's out of bounds at the moment, don't forget,' said

Alison. Aunt Win had made an announcement about this a few days ago, when the thaw had meant that the girls had started to explore the grounds more widely. The pool was still half-frozen, and beneath the chunks of ice floating on top were several feet of water. Around the edge of the pool the patio area, designed for deckchairs and poolside drinks, was slippery and wet. Until swimming lessons were to be properly organised for the summer months, the whole area had been firmly placed off-limits for the girls.

'Of course,' said Jeannie, 'but it'll be super in the summer won't it?' Somehow, they were all taking for granted that Four Winds was now established as a school and that the summer term would see them all back again after an Easter break. No one talked about the original idea that it was to be only for a few months while the twins' parents were in Japan.

'What do you suppose Aunt Win has planned for the summer, though?' asked Geraldine, following Jeannie's train of thought as she often did. 'Has she worked out lesson plans for the whole year, do you think?'

'The timetable is certainly all arranged for another term after this one, anyway,' said Elizabeth, overhearing. 'I know, because it's all on the computer. Mrs Ontwin said she didn't mind me telling you this, when I asked her about it the other day while helping out with the design system. She's had to make some long-term plans because otherwise it isn't fair on Miss Crisp and the school that rents us the science lab, and so on.'

'Mummy said she'd be able to tell us in her next letter about how long they are going to be in Japan,' said Geraldine, 'but I think she and Daddy are planning for us to be here with Aunt Win until the end of the school year anyway, whatever happens, partly because we've been telling them how much we're enjoying it. If they can't come back to England at Easter we'll either fly out to be with them in Japan, which would be tremendously exciting, or we'll go to Grandma's.'

'What about half-term?' asked Amanda. 'I'm going home, of course, and so's Alison – aren't you, Allie? Bernadette and Marie might be staying here but Evangeline's flying back to Switzerland.'

But at this point, further conversation was interrupted by the arrival of Miss Crisp and the start of an arithmetic lesson for the younger girls, while Alison, Gabriele and Elizabeth went into another room for a session on English poetry.

The next event was the arrival, a few days later, of Father Higgins' niece Amy Carruthers, with her parents. Amy was small and shy, rather pale and silent. She seemed somewhat overwhelmed by the other girls, whom she first met round the piano for a singing lesson. After a short talk in her office. Aunt Win had sent for Alison, who came down to fetch Mr and Mrs Carruthers and Amy and show them round the school. Amy answered only 'yes' and 'no' to friendly questions and didn't seem to want to talk at all, despite her mother's friendly encouragement. When they entered the music-room she shrank back at the sight of all the girls, who were learning a German song to the accompaniment of Mrs Hurry at the piano. After a brief break, Aunt Win told the class to carry on, as it didn't seem fair to Amy to subject her to a whole array of introductions and handshakes.

'Well, do you think you'll like this school, darling?' asked Mrs Carruthers as they made their way down the drive afterwards.

'Mmm yes, I think so,' said Amy hesitantly in a small voice. 'I liked the big fireplace, and the cakes and biscuits the big girls brought to us from the kitchen when they came in with their pinafores on. But it seems sort of ... big and noisy, doesn't it?'

'Does it?' asked her father anxiously. He exchanged glances with his wife. The school had struck them both as rather quiet and ordered. Amy had been away from school for a long time. Perhaps she had forgotten the normal noise and bustle of a busy girls' establishment.

'Would you be happy to be there all day, coming home to Daddy and me in the evenings?' asked her mother. 'We'll be staying with Uncle David for a couple of weeks more, you know, so you could try it out just as an experiment if you like. And Mrs Ontwin seems friendly and kind, doesn't she?'

'She's a bit – well – big and important,' said Amy, 'but I'm not going to be scared. I'll go to the school.'

She gave a great sigh and her parents both felt worried.

'Let's see how it goes for a few days,' said her father kindly. 'We only want what's best for our favourite girl.' He gave her a big hug,

Back at St Mary's presbytery, Mrs McMurdoch was preparing a tasty supper. She was a good cook and the smell coming from the kitchen was encouraging.

'How did the school visit go?' Father Higgins – Uncle David to Amy – was in a hurry as usual, just in from a visit to an old people's club and with things to prepare for his evening Confirmation class.

'We think we'll try it as an experiment anyway,' said his sister, helping him to stack and sort books as they spoke. 'I must say all the girls look very cheery and friendly. I suppose Mrs McMurdoch doesn't have a sewing machine? Even if it's only for a few days, I'd like to run up a uniform for Amy. She mustn't look different from the other girls.'

At the mention of his housekeeper, Father Higgins grinned. 'Oh, she's sure to have one,' he said. 'She's the soul of efficiency, that lady. And she'll be glad to help you do the sewing, too. She's always keen to find more to do.'

Mrs McMurdoch was a widow who had no children of her own and had worked for some years as matron at the nearby boys' school. When a small legacy meant that she no longer needed a full time job, she had decided to leave the school and devote herself to the Church and to village activities. But there was not really enough to fill up her time. Father Higgins joked about her but beneath her brisk and bossy exterior she was a kindly woman. It was small Amy who brought out the gentler side to her nature.

'Yes, we can make a really smart uniform from this material,' she said that evening in the presbytery kitchen, contemplating the roll of cloth that Mrs Carruthers had presented to her. 'It's a simple pattern and I can cut it out tonight and start sewing it tomorrow morning. Would you let me measure you, Amy? Just stand still and hold this end of the tape measure. Hmm, I'll have to adapt the pattern as you're rather smaller round the waist. The colour is nice, isn't it, especially with this lovely red ribbon near the hem? Would you like to help me with the sewing?'

In no time, she and Mrs Carruthers had become firm

friends, and young Amy felt relaxed and comfortable in her company. The three spent a couple of cosy afternoons in her small cottage, sewing the uniform and adding name-tapes to a red beret and scarf which Amy's father had bought from the shop in town where the other girls had bought theirs.

'This seems a popular colour this year,' said the girl at the counter as she wrapped up the garments. 'Someone came in the other day and bought four sets like this.'

'It's for Four Winds School,' said Mr Carruthers. 'You might get some more orders, too, as they're taking in more pupils.'

'Four Winds? I didn't know there was a school there,' said the girl. 'I thought it was that big hotel. They used to do posh dinners and dances there, didn't they? Fancy it being a school! Wouldn't have minded going there myself, with those lovely grounds.'

'Well, you can spread the word and send your younger sisters along!' joked Mr Carruthers. 'It seems to work well as a school, and my little Amy starts there after tomorrow. They specialise in music and languages, and the girls all seem very happy and well cared-for. They do cookery too – so the dinner tradition is still keeping up!'

'Fancy!' she said. 'Well I hope your girl enjoys it. I'll look out for the girls around the town in their red berets. I'm glad our store has become the official outfitters. We do sports gear too, you know. Tell the headmistress!'

Amy arrived with her uncle for school on Thursday morning. Aunt Win greeted them both at the front door and they went straight in to morning prayers. Each day one of the girls read a prayer or a passage from Scripture – usually in English but sometimes in one of their own languages if they preferred – and then everyone said the Lord's Prayer. Then, after a few notices, the day's lessons began. This morning Aunt Win quietly introduced Amy to everyone, with hand-shakes all round, before announcing that there'd be a netball game that afternoon in place of rounders, and that any delayed homework – this with a slight frown at Gabriele who was inclined to be lazy – had to be handed in by lunchtime. Then Amy joined the other younger girls for a French lesson, followed by drawing. At coffee-time she was amazed to see

66

two of the girls take crisp pinafores from a row hanging by the door and hurry downstairs, before a bell summoned everyone to a gathering round the fireplace.

'It's the kitchen-work rota,' explained Alison. 'We'll fit you in too. You'll be in a team with, let me see, Amanda and Marie I think. Elizabeth and I will work it out on the computer.'

Aunt Win had taken Geraldine quietly aside and asked her to take special care of Amy. This was a clever stroke, as it appealed to Geraldine's sense of leadership and of course also ensured that Jeannie and Amanda automatically became Amy's friends too. Geraldine delighted in showing Amy round the school.

'Here's where you hang your beret,' she announced importantly. 'And when you do kitchen duty, you have to wear a pinafore. Has one been got out for Amy yet?' she asked generally, as Bernadette and Joan were scrambling into theirs.

'Don't think so,' said Joan, calling it out over her shoulder as they were hurrying off to help lay the table for lunch, 'but there are loads of spares in the cupboard.'

Amy felt that she didn't want to be labelled as a new girl by not wearing one, so she trotted after Geraldine to the cupboard, but they were waylaid by Jeannie, eager to join in showing Amy everything. Lunch that day was to be sausages, beans and chips – a popular meal which, because the girls played a major part in planning all the menus, cropped up frequently. As always, it was punctuated by plenty of talk and laughter. Afterwards, the tour was resumed: 'And this is the garden, where we're each going to have our own plot as soon as the spring comes and we can start planting things. And this is where we're all going to help build a proper rockery and see if we can get a big fountain going. Come on Amy, don't lag behind!' It didn't perhaps occur to the twins that it was all a little overwhelming to a small girl who for weeks had been quietly at home with her parents, doing occasional lessons with visiting teachers and spending the afternoons with a book or a trip to the shops. That evening Amy went home exhausted and was even more silent than usual. It was Mrs McMurdoch, rather than her parents, who managed to discover from her what sort of a day she had had.

'Oh, they were all very nice, but it's so busy and complicated and I didn't ever get my pinafore,' said Amy. 'It made me feel a bit out of things.'

'But you enjoyed the lessons – and this girl Geraldine seems very nice?' asked Mrs Carruthers anxiously.

'Oh yes, awfully. And I do want to join in everything. But, well, it's just a lot of big new things all the time, one after another. And a lot of talking!'

Mrs McMurdoch was not one to let problems develop. Good-natured, if rather bossy, she decided in her own mind that perhaps Four Winds, if it couldn't organise a pinafore for a new girl, needed some help sorting itself out. So the next morning, without telling anyone, she bustled off in her smart green car and was soon knocking at the imposing front door.

'I've come to see the headmistress,' she announced briskly to Gabriele, who was on door-duty that day.

'Yes, of course. Er, please to sit down?' said Gabriele politely. 'I go fetch. Please to have your name?' When she was nervous she found English more difficult, but Mrs McMurdoch was charmed with this polite and nicely-behaved girl who showed good manners, and with the pleasant and well-ordered atmosphere as she sat in the panelled hall outside Aunt Win's office.

Unfortunately, this good impression did not last. Mrs Drummond staggered by with a big basket of washing, forgot something, hurried back, tripped and fell. Aunt Win came scurrying out of her office to help, a telephone rang insistently and somewhere upstairs a man's voice could be heard calling out something about making sure the stairs were clear as some heavy equipment was coming down. (It was Uncle Harry, busy with crucial arrangements for the final meeting of his team for the Africa trip.) Mrs McMurdoch ran to help Mrs Drummond and there was general chaos while it was established that she wasn't hurt, and meanwhile Aunt Win rushed to answer the telephone and then Uncle Harry humped some heavy Army equipment downstairs, calling out greetings as he passed.

Finally, order was established and Aunt Win was able to invite her visitor into her study.

'I really came just on a social call,' said Mrs McMurdoch.

68

'I'm Father Higgins' housekeeper and I just wondered if there was any extra help I could give here. I've been helping to look after little Amy while she's been staying with him.'

'Well!' Aunt Win was silenced for a moment. So this was the famous dragon! She was certainly a brisk, determined sort of lady. But there was a kindness in her manner and she had very expertly helped Mrs Drummond, and then insisted on calmly taking out the washing herself to hang it up while breezily introducing herself to Uncle Harry before coming into the office and apparently offering to give extra help to the school! Looking at her, Aunt Win's immediate feeling was one of sudden relief. It really would be useful to have an extra pair of hands.

'Well, it's very kind of you, but we really don't need ...' she started to say politely. But her honesty got the better of her. 'To be frank, things do get terribly hectic here,' she admitted. 'I was only saying to Father Higgins the other day that poor Mrs Drummond is overworked and it's not fair.' She paused and gave Mrs McMurdoch a grin. 'If it's a serious offer, I might take you up on it. Would you like some coffee?'

Half an hour later, having discussed Mrs McMurdoch's previous work as matron of a boy's school, and remembering Father Higgins' comment that his housekeeper didn't have enough work to do, Aunt Win had made an arrangement that Mrs McMurdoch would come in that very afternoon to finish off the laundry and sort out the bed-linen while Mrs Drummond was given a rest.

'And I'll get a pinafore out of the cupboard for Amy,' said Mrs McMurdoch determinedly, startling Aunt Win with her knowledge of the school's arrangements. 'And if there's any mending to be done, I'd be happy to take it home with me.'

And so another chapter in the history of Four Winds was born. Aunt Win checked out Mrs McMurdoch's references with the boys' school. 'Oh yes, we were actually extremely sorry to lose her,' said the headmaster wistfully. 'Rather strict with the boys when they mislaid their socks, but most kind to them when they were ill, and expert at getting them to wash their ears and pick up stray toffee papers around the place. Since she's left, we've found they've started to do all sorts of messy things like leaving chewing-gum in odd corners, which would never have happened in her day. We have a new matron now who is younger and less organised, and we do miss Mrs McMurdoch and rather envy you getting her.'

Aunt Win couldn't know, however, what a stir she caused by announcing at lunchtime that Mrs McMurdoch was going to be part of the school. The girls, remembering how Father Higgins had seemed so scared of her, were appalled at the prospect of her arriving. They didn't say anything to Aunt Win but immediately after lunch an indignation meeting was held in the schoolroom, headed by the twins and Amanda.

'We can't let this happen!' said Geraldine fiercely. 'It's always been so friendly and homelike here at Four Winds. We're not going to have a bossy dragon spoiling things!'

'Just let her try to start organising everything, and bossing us around!' said Jeannie. 'We won't let her. How can we get it stopped? Would Aunt Win listen if we all went to her and asked her to change her mind?'

'Gabriele say she seem a most kind, most friendly lady when Gabi answer the door to her this morning,' said Evangeline tentatively. 'Is perhaps ... is perhaps not so right to make a big decision? Maybe is better we all wait ... we see her?'

'No,' said Amanda. 'We simply can't. It isn't right to let Aunt Win make a big mistake like this. We all know what she's like: Father Higgins has told us. Even if she puts on a friendly front, she's going to be horrible once she's really installed.'

The discussion ended, however, without anything being really agreed, as Alison arrived to chivvy them out of doors. It was a rule that everyone always went outside after lunch to enjoy the fresh air, and normally everyone enjoyed this. The grounds were large and there was plenty to explore. The wintry trees looked beautiful against the sky and the breeze whirled freshness into everyone's lungs. Every day the grounds rang to happy sounds as games of hop-scotch or skipping formed up. The red scarves flashed brightly against the brown and grey of the winter gardens.

Today, however, there were important matters to discuss. Geraldine, Amy and Jeannie went off in a group, while Amanda and Bernadette found themselves still talking together about Mrs McMurdoch as they wandered down the drive.

Amanda skipped with pleasure in the fresh wind. The school grounds were most attractive, with interesting paths and gracious lawns. There was plenty of room to play and run about, and many pleasant little routes to follow to odd corners. On one stretch of paved courtyard the girls had drawn out squares for hop-scotch, and soon Geraldine, Jeannie and Amy were busy at the game, Amy forgetting her shyness in the fun of jumping and hopping about. She had not played with girls of her own age in the open air for far too long a time.

'Come and join us! It's just getting exciting!' called Geraldine, but Amanda was already out of earshot and, with Bernadette, was walking down one of the paths, still talking about the problem of the new matron.

'Of course, none of us has actually met her,' she said with honesty. 'At least, only Gabriele and then only for a few moments. It's perfectly possible that Father Higgins just doesn't get on with her. Perhaps she'll be different with girls from the way she is with him. But I still don't like the sound of her.'

'Perhaps we – how you say in English – send her to Coventry?' said Bernadette, who had read about such things in story-books. 'You know, that none of us speaks to her. We smile, yes, but we turn away and we do not pay attention.'

'It would be jolly rude, but perhaps we could sort of go half-way,' said Amanda thoughtfully. 'Just make it clear we won't be bossed around. Be cool and distant. Do what she says but very slowly. Get her annoyed with us so she'll give up and leave.'

Their walk had taken them to the edge of forbidden territory. Beyond them lay the patio area, fringed by trees and an attractive trellis, that marked the swimming pool. Both of them knew that this was out of bounds and they knew why. The swimming pool was deep and dangerous and its edges slippery with the grey slush of melting snow. But they couldn't resist, while no one was about, just going a bit nearer.

'Ooh, look!' cried Amanda. 'It's still got ice on the top. I wonder if it's thick enough to walk on?'

71

Neither girl said 'It's out of bounds', although that thought was in the front of their minds. Hardly daring to look at one another, they ran quickly forward. The pool was flanked on one side by a low, pleasant building with changing-rooms and a café area. It looked bleak and neglected in the wintry weather. It seemed hard to imagine people sitting there enjoying drinks and watching the bathers.

'Look, the ice is all breaking up and floating about,' said Amanda, stretching out her foot to touch the nearest chunk. Great grey slabs of the ice moved against one another, while around the edges of the pool the water, full of dead leaves and bits of wind-blown rubbish, slopped and gurgled. It was satisfying to make the ice move a bit more. She gave one good-sized chunk a shove, wobbling dangerously near the edge as she did so.

'It is dirty, not so good for swimming,' observed Bernadette, peering down at it. 'Maybe frogs and weeds too. I wonder ...'

'Amanda! What are you doing here?' The voice was booming, loud, clear and very angry. It was Aunt Win's and it came from just behind them. Swiftly, the girls turned round. There was their headmistress, watching them from the school building across the patio! Amanda had speedily drawn back the foot that had been prodding the ice and now she and Bernadette retreated, looking hastily for the path to make a quick getaway. But Aunt Win was too quick for them. In a trice she had darted out through the French windows.

'Did you, or did you not, know that this area is out of bounds?' she asked. 'And did you stop to think why I had made that rule?' She was so angry that her voice had a quiver in it. She had looked out of the window quite casually, while working in the room beyond, which she was planning to turn into an art room. She had seen with horror Amanda putting out her foot across the deep water. Across her mind had darted with the speed of lightning a picture of the child falling into the pool, struggling and gasping under the ice, submerged, drowning.

'No, we ... I ... er ...' Both girls spoke at once but no proper words came out. Bernadette burst into tears. 'Sorry. Oh, so sorry,' she blurted out. She had never seen a grown-up

72

look as scared and white-faced as Mrs Ontwin, and it suddenly dawned on her that the headmistress was not being cross and nasty but had been terrified for their very lives. The same thought suddenly occurred to Amanda too, and she covered her face with her hands as a gulping sob came up.

'Sorry? I should think you are sorry!' Aunt Win was still for a moment almost incapable of speech, as she propelled the girls down the path in front of her. 'Can you imagine what might have happened if – oh goodness, you did scare me.' They were away from the pool now and she swivelled them round to look at her.

'I don't make rules in this house for girls to break,' she said. Her voice was steady now. 'And I don't make them just to be boring and disagreeable. If you had stopped to think about it for just one moment it might have occurred to you that the reason the pool is out of bounds is because it is twelve feet deep and covered in treacherous ice.' She paused for a moment to let the thought sink in. 'Well, you're going to have time to think about it,' she said. 'At tea-time this afternoon, when the others take their break, you'll stay in the schoolroom. You'll write out thirty times in English and thirty times in French, "I must not go near the swimming pool area." You'll hand the lines in to me before supper. I'll be waiting in my room for you.'

And with that she shooed them off back towards the house. Both girls were in tears. They didn't want to have to explain to the others what all the fuss was all about. It felt terrible to be in disgrace, and suppose Mrs Ontwin never trusted them again? It was the start of an unhappy afternoon.

It also meant that the talk about dealing with the problem of The Dragon rather petered out, and only half-hearted attempts were made to revive it. At tea-time Amanda and Bernadette, hardly looking at one another, got out sheets of paper and prepared to write their lines. They felt silly and conspicuous. Everyone knew why they were staying up in the schoolroom instead of joining the cosy group by the fire. Writing the lines didn't actually take long, although it was boring. Amanda needed Bernadette's help in working out how the sentence should read in French. They were hard at work when Gabriele and Marie, on duty that day, brought up their mugs of tea and toasted buns. They gave them sympathetic glances but didn't say anything.

The lines were done by the time everyone trooped back upstairs, and both girls rather wanted to take them down to Aunt Win right away and get the matter over with, but they couldn't. There was a singing lesson and then geography. Only when finally the buzzer went marking the end of afternoon school could they hurry down to the office by the main front door.

Standing outside, they both felt suddenly nervous.

'You knock,' said Bernadette.

'No, you,' said Amanda. 'Well, all right, both of us together.'

Aunt Win was sitting at her desk as usual, some papers in front of her. She looked up as the girls came in, and then held out her hand for the lines. She frowned slightly as she looked them through to see that they had been done correctly. Then, with a swift movement, she dropped them lightly on to the desk top in front of her.

'The matter's over,' she said. 'I know that from now on you are two girls on whom I can specially rely for obedience and trustworthiness.' And, in what was swiftly to become a school tradition, she held out her hand across the desk and each girl in turn shook it warmly. 'Amanda, please,' were her last words as the girls left the room, 'before you rush into things, do think beforehand.' These were words that Amanda was to remember later.

Chapter 8

'Well, we still haven't decided what to do about The Dragon.' It was the next morning at coffee break and, after a swift glance round to make sure no teacher was listening, the girls were holding a revived indignation session. Only Geraldine and Amy were absent, taking trays back to the kitchen.

'We don't really, absolutely, know that she's a dragon yet,' said Alison uncomfortably, conscious that Amanda was taking the lead on this and feeling that, being older, she ought to assume some responsibility. 'It was only some things that Father Higgins said. We ought to give her the benefit of the doubt.'

'And I'm not going to be party to a silly campaign of being nasty to her,' interjected Elizabeth. Alison looked at her, surprised and with new respect. Elizabeth might have slightly punk hair and adore pop music but she talked sense at times. 'Nor am I, then,' said Joan loyally, pleased that her older sister was taking the initiative. 'I think we ought to be friendly. This school is a friendly place, and there are so few of us it would be horrible to start making a nasty atmosphere.'

'All very well for you, you won't be much affected,' said Amanda. 'You two are day-girls. It won't be your bedrooms she'll be endlessly wanting to tidy up, or your hair she'll be nagging you to tie back, or your hankies she'll be wanting to count up.' Immediately after saying this, she felt bad about it. The two Hurry girls were as much a part of the school as all the others. In fact, increasingly since Elizabeth's miracles with the computer, they had become an indispensable part.

Gabriele immediately came to their rescue. 'As to that,' she said, 'I think both Elizabeth and Joan see things more clearly. And perhaps too, as they have lived in the village, they know more of Mrs – what is her name – McMurder? McMumm? – and know that she is not really so unfriendly.'

'Yes, well, that's perfectly true, she ...' Joan started to say, but it was lost in the general laughter at Gabriele's muddle over the new matron's name. McMurder! It was perfect! The younger girls shouted with glee. It became impossible to talk further. But as the school returned to lessons upstairs, the three older girls, talking together, came to an agreement that they would not allow any silly unpleasantness to arise over Mrs McMurdoch's arrival. They would try to find a moment to communicate this to the younger ones, and if necessary take a firm stand about it.

That afternoon Elizabeth again gave some help to Aunt Win at the computer. Aunt Win was torn between being pleased that here was an aspect of Four Winds that Elizabeth seemed to enjoy and a real concern that it was taking her away from her lessons.

'In a lot of schools ...' Elizabeth had been going to say 'In proper, big, modern schools' but checked herself in time. '... there are computer sessions for everyone, and all the pupils use the computers as a matter of course.'

'I know,' said Aunt Win, worried, 'and if we could just master this one then everyone could take a turn on it, and of course eventually we could buy more, when funds run to it, and even perhaps establish a small computer room.'

'There is that one other computer,' Elizabeth pointed out, 'the one they used to have for hotel registrations, that's now in the cupboard. That could be up and running again for routine work, I should think, if you'd let me have a go at it. Look, do you want me to show you how this spell-check thing works, just once again?'

The two chatted as they worked together, and soon Aunt Win was looking at the unused computer and agreeing that it could be brought back into service. 'But we'll need someone to help us get it going,' frowned Elizabeth, looking at its instruction manual. 'It's been dismantled in a rather muddled away and I'm not sure I can tackle it alone. Look, here's a business card stuck on the side, with a number to ring for help. Can we do that? I think the firm just sends someone along.'

'Yes, let's do that,' said Aunt Win thoughtfully. Already she could see the small room on the opposite side of the hall being handed over to the girls for some computer work. Perhaps they might like to run a school magazine? Produce programmes for the end-of-term concert? Many possibilities loomed. She was also thinking of something else. Elizabeth's whole approach and manners had improved since they had discovered her interest in this. It was obviously part of the key to the girl's whole attitude towards Four Winds. Standing there, leafing through the computer manual, her habitual sullen look was gone. She looked smart in her blue-grey uniform dress with its double-band of red velvet ribbon a few inches above the hem. A few days earlier, Aunt Win had confiscated a silly and sordid magazine that Elizabeth had brought into the school. They had talked about it and Elizabeth had admitted that it didn't really represent ideas she found valuable or real. It had been established that such material would not appear again at Four Winds. Strangely, this assertion of authority on the part of her headmistress had steadied and helped Elizabeth. Her attitude towards many things was changing.

Aunt Win was aware that, until very recently, almost every day had brought a comment from Elizabeth that she 'wouldn't be staying at Four Winds much longer' or that she 'couldn't wait to get back to her real school'. Poor Mrs Hurry had been embarrassed, hurt and anxious about it all, and at times almost incapable of handling her difficult teenage daughter. Now at last a key seemed to have been turned in a difficult lock.

'I'll be telephoning the computer firm immediately,' said Aunt Win as they stacked papers away. 'You've really got a talent at this, Elizabeth. You're making a tremendous contribution to the school by your initiative on this.'

Her call to the firm brought a response the very next morning. An imposing car drew up outside Four Winds and a tall Indian gentleman got out. He introduced himself at the front door with his card – Mr Deva of Compactor Computers.

Marie politely let him in and knocked on Aunt Win's door.

'We received your call, and as I happened to be in the area myself, I thought I would call personally,' he said. 'Of course, this hotel has been one of our most important clients. It's a real pleasure to be in Four Winds again. I have enjoyed some pleasant meals here but ...' he looked around in some puzzlement. Aunt Win's teaching diplomas hung on the wall. Brochures about school equipment were scattered across her desk and an enlarged timetable, with sections clearly labelled 'Art', 'French', 'Needlework', etc., took up much of the notice-board along one wall. 'This is all very different!' he finished, in some confusion.

Aunt Win laughed. 'Of course,' she said. 'I should have explained. My husband inherited this place from his aunt and we have closed the hotel and turned it into a school. We still need the computers but for rather different purposes. I'm so glad you are familiar with us of old. Would you like some coffee? The computer that needs fixing is out in the hall. I was thinking of establishing a computer room across on the other side.'

'A school!' he said, as they crossed the hall together. 'Well, that's astonishing. Who would take on a school today – so much work and responsibility?' They stopped to enjoy the fire for a few moments.

'Well, it all really started by accident,' said Aunt Win, waving her hand vaguely in a gesture to include the stairs going up to the schoolroom and the girls' coats and berets hanging in a neat line on hooks by the door. 'My two nieces needed somewhere to stay while their parents went to Japan, and then a friend of theirs came along and brought a cousin ... and there were my pupils from abroad and – well – the thing just grew!'

'Well, it seems splendid!' he said warmly. 'And what a beautiful place for girls to study and grow up together. Goodness me, it seems no time at all since I was last here having sherry in this very hall before a local luncheon. Four Winds has always played a big part in local life, you know,' he added. 'The Rotary Club used to meet here and it was always the place to use for smart dinners and meetings. But I know the number of visitors has dwindled. Other local firms have felt it too. It's the fault of this ugly motorway, and there are so many other attractions in prettier villages.'

'Well, we'd like Four Winds to help bring new life into the village if we can,' said Aunt Win. 'At least it means there will be young people around. My girls have already been out skating a lot, and I'd like them to join the ballet classes in the village hall – at least, the younger ones. Then there's riding and sports of course.' They were still chatting comfortably as they carried the computer into the room allocated and worked together at setting it up. Mr Deva proved as able a teacher of computers as Elizabeth, and expressed himself satisfied when it was working smoothly. 'Of course, in a way it's a pity as it means I can't sell you a newer one,' he said. 'But if you are really serious about teaching your pupils how to use our machines, then I can leave you some brochures.'

He was interrupted by a loud buzzer, and soon a chattering crowd of girls came busily down the stairs, settling themselves round the fire, talking and laughing. Mr Deva couldn't help smiling at the charming and cosy scene. He was even more impressed when two more girls came up from the kitchen bearing pots of coffee and politely offered some refreshment to their headmistress and visitor.

'No thank you, we've already had some,' he said. 'But are you pupils too? And did you make these biscuits?'

'Yes, of course we are, and the biscuits came from our cookery lesson,' said Amanda. 'They're the favourite ones, though we make lemon and oatmeal ones too, and next week we're doing shortbread from a Scottish recipe.'

'Delightful. Well, I congratulate you,' said Mr Deva, turning to Aunt Win. 'It's a most happy and beautiful school.' He was evidently thinking of something. 'Is it just a small establishment or are you still accepting pupils?' he asked diffidently. 'Only a thought has just occurred to me.'

Aunt Win almost knew what was coming. It was a pattern that had started to repeat itself. Girls from France and Austria! Father Higgins' niece! It seemed as if the school simply was a magnet attracting pupils.

'It's my daughters,' explained Mr Deva. 'My wife and I have been unhappy about them for some time. To be honest, we do not like what we have seen of so many English schools. It

79

is all right at the primary level, but for older ones some things are just not right. Scruffy clothing and lots of loud music. Meeting boyfriends at lunchtime. Little respect for traditions or religion. Picking up so many silly ideas that the teachers don't seem to check. It's not what we want for our girls. After much thought we decided a few months ago to send our eldest daughter back home to school in India. She is staying with her grandparents there but I know she is not happy. We get letters and telephone calls. Of course the culture is so very different. And now the younger one is making a fuss and says she doesn't want to go. We had planned for her to join Meena at the Indian school next term. I wonder ... could I make an appointment to come with my wife and talk about all of this?'

'Delighted,' said Aunt Win. 'We certainly have room for some more pupils. And it is true that here at Four Winds we are able to make a family atmosphere that avoids some of the difficulties many modern schools encounter. We want to be at the service of parents. If you feel your daughters could benefit from what we have to offer, then they could certainly come here.'

They talked further about it and Mr Deva said that he would be bringing his wife round to the school as soon as possible. 'We might bring Renu – my younger girl – too,' he said. 'She would be only too happy to take a morning off school! We have boys in the family too, but they are older now and well settled. One works with me – this is a family firm you know, and we own it – and the other two are away at university and both doing extremely well. One plans to be a doctor.'

By mid-afternoon, a telephone call had settled an appointment for the Deva family to view the school. Aunt Win marked it in her diary, but by the time they came a crisis had blown up.

It was all about Mrs McMurdoch, of course. Partly because they were all so fond of Father Higgins, the youngest girls had got it into their heads that he really had been persecuted by his housekeeper, although all that he had ever said about her had been in a light-hearted way. Young Amy Carruthers had not been present at any of the discussions that had taken place on the subject, and would quickly have been able to set matters to rights if she had. She knew extremely well that 'The Dragon' was not so ferocious. Indeed, she was spending many cosy evenings with her in the presbytery kitchen, watching her mend some of the Four Winds tablecloths and make plans for taking up work at the school in a few days' time. She was simply a lady who needed plenty to do! But no one asked Amy about her and no one thought to work out that the little girl would have been a good source of information on the subject.

Realising that the older girls were not going to join in any planned campaign, Amanda, Bernadette, Evangeline and Marie were leaders in the scheme. The twins were more reluctant, and Joan had already made clear that she wanted no part of it. She didn't know Mrs McMurdoch well but had seen her bustling round the village. It didn't seem right to start labelling her as a dragon without first meeting her properly.

'We won't talk to her,' decreed Amanda. 'And we won't answer her questions. If possible, we'll confuse and annoy her. We'll make extra work – mix up clothes from the laundry and that sort of thing. She'll soon be glad to get away from us.'

It was not so easy as it seemed. Arriving in time for morning prayers, Mrs McMurdoch was introduced with handshakes all round, and Alison was invited to give her a formal tour of the school while the others were starting their lessons. Alison found her friendly and efficient. It had to be admitted that the school needed a matron. Most of the bedrooms were untidy. No one inspected them regularly or checked that the windows were open to ensure a good airing or that all clothes for washing were brought promptly down to the laundry-room. Some of the bathrooms were steamy, unaired and even grubby. Overworked Mrs Drummond had tried to get the girls to accept responsibility for certain tasks but it had not been successful.

'And are all your clothes marked, so there's no confusion when they come back from being washed?' asked Mrs McMurdoch. Alison looked awkward. The general scramble for clothes was one of the less well-ordered arrangements at

Four Winds. Things tended to be left in a big pile and everyone just rummaged to grab their own garments as they needed them. It was evident that this was all going to change. Name-tags and neat labels, proper systems and tidy piles of clothes were going to be the order for the future. It had to be admitted that it would make things easier and waste less time.

By mid-morning coffee the new matron – Aunt Win had announced that 'Matron' was to be the title by which she was known – was well settled. She took her coffee-break in the kitchen with the Drummonds and they relaxed and laughed together, swapping village news. But it seemed odd that the girls, who had shaken hands so pleasantly that morning, turned their backs and did not smile or greet her as they came in with trays to take upstairs. Nor did they respond to her friendly greeting as they returned to wash up. At lunchtime Gabriele asked her politely if she was enjoying her first day, and they had a pleasant chat. But from Marie and Bernadette, chatting on the stairs, she got only cold looks and glares, and from Amanda, who had been doing some sewing and was trying to thread a needle, a direct snub when she tried to help.

'Oh well, perhaps they are just shy,' she thought, though rather troubled. Amy, on the other hand, had danced up to her with glee and was now talking quite happily about the prospect of being a boarder at the school when her parents left Uncle David's house in a few days' time. Having a matron on hand who was already a friend made all the difference.

'Come and see the work I've been doing,' she said as the pupils took off their coats and scarves after their midday break. 'I've started a project all about electricity. And you must see my lovely history chart with all the kings and queens on it.' She led the matron upstairs, and as they passed Amanda there was another glare. In the schoolroom Evangeline, whose place was next to Amy's, deliberately got up and walked away.

'It's puzzling,' said Mrs McMurdoch to herself, settling down with brushes and scourers to tackle a grimy bathroom. 'Is it something I've accidentally said? I hope I haven't criticised anything – though these taps could do with a shine and these rings on the bath are disgraceful.'

The unpleasantness went on all afternoon. It became even worse in the evening. Matron was to live in at the school, going home only one night a week to her own cottage. This was a big sacrifice as she loved her little home, which she would now only be able to enjoy properly in the holidays. She had left St Mary's presbytery in spick-and-span order, with a freezer full of food and a team of helpers organised to arrange Father Higgins' meals whenever he needed them. She would visit regularly to make sure all was well.

Her room at Four Winds was comfortable and pleasant. She shared supper with Aunt Win and Uncle Harry and called out a cheerful 'hello' to a group of girls sitting round the hall fire as she made her way to her own room with an armful of sewing.

'Don't say anything!' she heard Amanda hiss. 'She's The Dragon – remember?' Marie had almost automatically risen politely but she now sat down again and turned her back on the matron. Evangeline tossed her head and appeared deep in a book. Feeling snubbed, Matron walked on. She met Jeannie in the corridor upstairs. They were both trying to pass through a door at the same time. Jeannie held the door open for her but it was done without a smile, without any gesture of friendship. Hurt and slightly bewildered, Matron reached her own room with some relief.

Chapter 9

The same coldness continued the next morning. There was no 'good morning' from Jeannie, Bernadette and Geraldine as they passed Matron in the corridor on their way to breakfast. She greeted them but got a poor response. A few moments later Gabriele gave her a pleasant smile, for which she was grateful, but somehow the day still seemed to be getting off to a wrong start.

But she must not delay. There was work to be done and she had promised to help Mrs Drummond in the kitchen and enjoy her own breakfast there before dealing with the problem of the bedrooms. The girls had fallen into the habit of leaving their rooms in a mess. An announcement would have to be made about this and a system installed. Mrs Ontwin had already agreed about this and was rather keen on it. Every girl would have to strip her bed, open wide the windows and tidy the room before going to breakfast. After the meal, each would make her bed and leave the room immaculate. There would be inspections during the morning. Matron was even thinking about keeping a chart and awarding a prize for the tidiest room at the end of term.

Thinking about all this made Matron bustle. She stopped to pick up a sweet paper from the floor. Litter! That would have to stop too. Pocketing it, and making a mental note to check that there were enough waste-paper baskets around, she headed for the stairs.

Here Amanda, who was in a hurry, swerved to avoid her. Amanda was in stockinged feet. Last night she had kicked off her shoes as they all sat companionably round the hall fire.

She had got her feet wet running in the garden at tea-time and had stretched out her toes to the warm blaze and enjoyed the cosy feeling as she sat chatting with the other girls. Later she had gone up to bed without bothering to put her shoes on, and was now hurrying to fetch them.

She almost collided with Matron at the head of the stairs and, in her anxiety to hurry past her so that she would not have to say 'good morning', she took a wrong footing, slipped and fell. She was too quick and her feet slithered on the carpet. She gave a sharp cry as she tumbled downwards, knocked herself against the bannisters, rolled over and finally collapsed in a heap halfway down the stairs.

She had a jabbing pain in her foot. Everything felt confused. She heard herself shouting 'Ow!' and there were lots of people running. A confusion of voices.

'She's all right. She's not unconscious!'

'What happened, Amanda?'

'Is anything broken?'

They all hurried towards her from the kitchen and from the landing, meeting around her half-way down the stairs. She was lying awkwardly and her foot felt very uncomfortable. 'I'm all right!' she said and tried to get up. Matron was there, and suddenly she loomed not as terrifying or dragon-like but as rather reassuring.

'Don't move, dear,' she said. 'Just a moment. Let me see.'

It was not as serious as it had first appeared. The fall had not damaged her back or legs, although she was later to find herself very bruised. Apart from a cut on her hand, where she had stretched out to save herself and knocked it against a corner of the bannisters, she had slashed open the underside of her foot – blood had splashed dramatically up on the wall and across the stair – and had broken one toe. Amanda shouted out as she stared at it. There it was, sticking out at right angle from a big hole in her tights, weird, bizarre and horrible.

'Ow! Look! My foot!' Until now she had merely been in shock from the fall, but quite suddenly she burst into tears.

Everyone moved swiftly to help her. Already Aunt Win, summoned from breakfast by the shouting, was at her side. Once it was established that her foot was the only real injury,

Matron helped her to a big armchair in the hall. The other girls, gathered in a chattering crowd offering help and telling each other what had happened, were gently shooed out of the way.

Matron knew that this was a minor injury – the toe would simply be pulled back into place and strapped with sticking-plaster to the one next to it and allowed to mend – but it probably ought to be x-rayed. The cut underneath the foot was quite deep and ought to be stitched.

'I'll get you to the hospital,' she said briskly. 'Could someone get her coat? And a scarf – it's cold. And a shoe for the other foot – that'll make it easier to get her in and out of the car.' She smoothed Amanda's hair and passed her a hankie produced by Alison, saying quietly comforting things.

Soon a taxi was at the door and Amanda was able to hobble out to it, using her heel and leaning on the twins. The sight of her foot, with its toe still sticking out at a crazy angle, struck her anew as she was carried across the hall and she went into renewed floods of tears. Matron settled her into the car and they swept off down the drive.

People rally round well in a crisis. In no time, Alison was supervising a group cleaning up the mess on the stairs and removing all traces of blood from the big armchair and from the route where Amanda had been carried across the hall. A faint, but not unpleasant, tingling smell of disinfectant was soon all that remained. Breakfast went ahead as usual, every-one talking about what had happened and speculating about how things were going at the hospital. Soon Matron tele-phoned. All was well. Amanda was in the casualty department and would soon receive treatment.

So while lessons began at Four Winds, Amanda was begin-ning to find the adventure quite exciting.

'Aren't you lucky having Mrs McMurdoch as your school matron?' said the x-ray nurse chattily, helping her into a wheelchair. 'She's done so much for this hospital over the years: run our League of Friends and got the little boys at that school where she used to work – Medsham Manor wasn't it? – to come and sing to our elderly patients with little concerts. All the books and magazines in the coffee bar where people sit to wait – in fact the coffee bar itself with all its nice chairs and the proper equipment to make real coffee and nice rolls and cakes – all came from the League, under her leadership.'

It emerged, too, that over the years Matron had had to ferry various small boys into the hospital for minor injuries – a twisted ankle from the football field and once a broken wrist after a fall from a tree – so she was recognised as belonging to the world of schools and children.

'She runs first-aid classes every Autumn in the village. She got her own certificate some years ago as part of training to work as a school matron and thought she'd pass on her skills,' said the doctor as he prepared to stitch up Amanda's foot. 'She roped me in, too. I'm one of the team that tests people at the end of the course, and I must say I think she does a good job. It does help if people know what to do in an emergency so we don't get patients brought in here who have been made worse through bungled attempts to help. Now, this might hurt just a little bit as I give you an injection, but it means that when I actually stitch you up you won't feel a thing.'

Having an injection in your toe is nasty, but once everything was over, her foot strapped up and a special shoe put on so that she could shuffle around, Amanda began to feel much better and rather important. She was also tremendously hungry. While they were waiting for the taxi to take them back, she and Matron had hot fresh coffee and cheese rolls in the coffee-bar.

'OK now?' Matron grinned at her across the table. Amanda hadn't noticed that her clear grey eyes were smiling and kind.

'Yes, thanks. I say, I'm, er, awfully grateful to you for giving up your whole morning like this. And on your first day, too!' Deep down inside, Amanda knew that the whole fault for the accident had been hers. If she hadn't been so determined to avoid Matron and not have to say 'good morning' to her, she would never have fallen. It all seemed so silly now. It was really quite hard to find much to dislike about this quiet, if rather efficient, lady who was rooting in her handbag for cash for the coffee and looking around to check on the whereabouts of Amanda's crutches.

'Hallo! They told me you were here! Has there been an

adventure at Four Winds?' The speaker was Father Higgins, hurrying up with a bundle of papers under his arm. Amanda automatically tried to get up to greet him, but suddenly found it was more uncomfortable than she had realised. Bother! She was going to be slowed down in everything she did for days, probably weeks, to come. But she gave him a big smile and was even able to greet him in Latin, as they did at his lessons.

'Salve! Ut vales?' She could see that Matron was quite impressed, but that was as far as she could go in Latin so she switched to English. 'I fell down the stairs. It was all my own fault, really. And I've had an x-ray and been stitched up and they've pulled my broken toe across and strapped it to the next one. Would you like to see?'

'No thanks, I'll take your word for it! In answer to your greeting: Salvete! Optime, valeo. It's my day for making hospital visits, and while I was upstairs someone mentioned that you were here, Matron'. He gave Mrs McMurdoch her proper school title now for the first time since she had stopped being his housekeeper. 'Lots of people will want to say hello to you. Have you managed to talk to any of your League of Friends team? They're all looking forward to seeing you at the Annual Meeting.'

Matron patted Canis and beamed up at Father Higgins.

'Have you time to join us for a hot drink? We're waiting for the taxi but they did warn us it might be a while.'

'Not really. Well ...' he looked at his watch, 'yes, it actually might be nice, as I haven't had anything all morning.' He checked himself hurriedly as Mrs McMudoch looked concerned. 'Yes, I know you did leave me lots of food at home, and I assure you everything's fine there, but I was rushed here early before breakfast as someone needed me, and I haven't managed to stop for a break.' He rummaged in his pocket for change. 'No, don't get up, I'll get it for myself. Another cup for each of you?'

So there was Amanda, sitting down with Father Higgins and The Dragon, all three chatting away as if they had been friends for years! He asked about the school, told Matron that he thought all the girls would turn out as excellent Latin scholars, and got her laughing as he explained the idea of having a Latin lunch. They all giggled over what the menu might be – what did the ancient Romans eat when they weren't having full-scale banquets? – and she told him how impressed she was with the beautiful setting at Four Winds.

'It's a friendly place, too,' he told her, 'but I expect you've already found that. A welcome for everyone – a family feeling. Lots of smiling. They're all helping to invent a new school so every single day there's something different happening to make it all work.'

Amanda suddenly felt uncomfortable. A welcome. Smiling. Everyone helping one another. And she had been the leader in a campaign to make their new matron feel particularly unwelcome. When Mrs McMurdoch got up to take the cups and plates back to the counter she turned on Father Higgins.

'Why did you tell us she was a dragon?' she said. 'We all thought she was going to be horrible. We even …' She was going to say 'We even had a campaign to be beastly to her' but checked herself.

Father Higgins looked at her. Perhaps he half-understood what she was going to say. 'If I said anything that would have make you dislike her in advance, that was wrong of me,' he said seriously. 'She a nice person. She's rather efficient, as no doubt you'll find. You won't get away with much! She'll nag you in making sure your foot heals properly and scurry around making sure every part of the school is shining clean and everything functions perfectly. And I don't mind betting she gets you up here singing to the old folk and starts you all off on a First Aid course in the village, and goodness knows what else! Give that woman a job to do. and she does it thoroughly.'

He looked again at Amanda's troubled face. 'If I led any of you into a wrong understanding of her, then the fault was entirely mine,' he said. 'I mean that. I shouldn't have said anything thoughtless.' He paused and there was a silence. He sighed and frowned to himself. 'Well, I must make amends. We must all give Matron McMurdoch a really good welcome and start her life at Four Winds on a really happy note. I'll take the lead, as it was my responsibility in the first place.' He held out his hand. 'Will you shake on it?' Amanda grinned shyly and then put out her hand and they pumped up and down solemnly.

Matron came back and they grinned at one another as she bustled around helping.

'Look after that foot,' said Father Higgins to Amanda. 'I'll be along for Latin tomorrow. Valete!'

'Nice man,' said Matron as they went out to the car. 'We're lucky to have him as the parish priest here. He works hard. But I think the Bishop will move him one day, as he really deserves a bigger parish and more important work. He's really quite a scholar, you know.'

Back at Four Winds there was quite a welcome. Everyone wanted to know if Amanda was all right, and she was not short of helpers to manoeuvre her upstairs and help her to her place in the schoolroom. The first thing she did was to whisper to everyone that Matron had been super 'We were wrong about her,' she said. 'She's really nice. Tell you all about it at break.'

And, walking with difficulty on her crutches up and down the main path at break time, Amanda told the other girls what had happened at the hospital, and about her conversation with Father Higgins. What was rather humiliating was the reaction of small Amy.

'Matron's super!' she said indignantly. 'If you'd only asked me, I could have told you! I've been seeing her every day for nearly a week, as she's been Uncle David's – Father Higgins' – housekeeper, and she's been really kind to me!'

Indignation and a strong sense of justice had given her a new voice. The shyness was gone. 'Just let anyone be horrible to Mrs McMurdoch!' she said. 'I'll be her friend, whatever anyone says, ever. And I'm going to be a boarder here now, to make sure she's all right and properly looked after. If any of you are nasty to her – well – well – you'll have to answer to me, that's all!'

It was hard not to laugh at this small person, angry and determined that justice should prevail. But the other girls assured her that the matter was settled. Matron was one of the team now, and even if they found her bustling ways annoying at times, they were making her welcome.

'League of Friends at the hospital, Father Higgins' church, First Aid in the village – it's all a bit much, but that's her way and we'll have to live with it,' Geraldine declared. 'She's taking things gently with us, anyhow. She hasn't invented lots of new rules or stopped us having fun yet.'

'I don't think she's going to do that,' said Amanda, who was fast becoming Matron's closest ally. 'I think she'll make us pick up litter and tidy our rooms and so on, but I don't mind that. And if she wants us to go and sing up at the hospital, well, that might be quite fun. Did I tell you that she got the boys from her old school doing that?'

Next day Father Higgins came to take the Latin lessons as usual – and as usual it was hilarious and fun. He stayed for lunch and, before they ate suggested that they all give three cheers for their new matron who had coped so well yesterday in getting Amanda to hospital, and who would be looking after them all. They gave them willingly, while Matron McMurdoch blushed and looked embarrassed but happy. It was a very cheerful school that settled down to hamburgers and pomo terrestria assa (chips!).

Chapter 10

The next event, of course, was the arrival of Mr and Mrs Deva with Renuka – Renu for short – who was to be Four Winds' next new pupil. There was never really any doubt about that from the moment they walked through the door. Renu – who was easily going to be the most beautiful girl in the school, with her dark eyes and glossy almost blue-black hair – seemed happy with everything, and her parents were delighted.

'This is just what we had in mind when we were looking for a school,' said Mrs Deva quietly, after a tour of the bedrooms, schoolroom, music department, grounds and kitchen. 'It is comfortable, well-ordered, friendly and cheerful. The girls seem to work hard – Renu hasn't done German or Latin before, so that will be new for her – but they seem to enjoy themselves.'

'I'm only sorry that we didn't know about this school before we sent Meena off to India,' said Mr Deva, referring to his older daughter with some anxiety. 'I don't like the girls to be separated. They have always been good friends. I had always planned that they spend their schooldays together. Well, we must see what can be done about next term. She already has her return ticket and I know she is looking forward to the holidays.'

Renu had already chosen the place where she wanted to sit in the schoolroom, and even at the lunch table. She had peered at the timetable on Aunt Win's notice-board and been pleased with the friendly welcome in the kitchen and the way the girls helped with cookery and enjoyed good food. The meals at her present school were dreary and unappetising.

The family lived not far away. Renu had not left home before and it was arranged that she would be a weekly boarder so that she could go back at weekends. This pleased Aunt Win as it meant that she could perhaps be a link between the boarders and the day-girls. If there were any special events at weekends, an arrangement could easily be made for Renu to stay.

She suddenly thought about morning prayers.

'You must tell me what you want for Renu,' she said. 'She certainly need not join in Christian prayers if it's against your family's religious tradition. As the school grows, it may be necessary to make arrangements for different pupils. Please let me know what you'd like done about that.'

'We've already talked about it at home,' said Mr Deva. 'We'd like Renu to take part in prayers every morning. We are Hindus and we respect all religions. One of the things we have disliked about her present school is that they seem to have no place for religion at all. They behaved as though they were pagans! The teachers appeared to dislike the subject, and although we asked about Christianity they were just vague about it. We can teach our daughter the Hindu faith at home, and already she is well formed in it, but we would like her to learn about Christianity while she is at school, along with the other subjects that we cannot teach her. So we would like her to join with the others each morning. Of course she will have her private prayers in her own room, and we will remind her about that.'

Renu was more interested in domestic details. 'Will I have a big starched apron like the other girls?' she asked. 'And learn to talk French at lunchtimes?' At present, some of this seemed something between a huge joke and a most exciting challenge.

'Yes, of course,' laughed Aunt Win. 'They keep inventing new traditions all the time, I'm afraid! We'll have to see what you come up with. And French and German meals, yes, and everything. On Thursday mornings we even greet each other in Latin and I found Mrs Drummond muttering about ancient Roman lunches a while ago. You'll enjoy it all here, I think, but be prepared for it to be a bit different from your old school! Friendly, though, and full of surprises!' Renu's answer was a wide grin. She was looking forward to life at Four Winds.

There was further talk and finally it was agreed that Renu would start later that week. Mrs Deva started to enquire about uniforms. 'Your girls look very smart in their nice pinafore-dresses, and I see the red hats and scarves hanging up. What else is there to buy?'

'Nothing, really,' said Aunt Win. 'The uniform is a new arrangement. I'm afraid we can only supply the cloth, as we've been doing our own sewing. I can give you the name of the shop where we bought the berets.'

'I'll get a tailor in town to make Renu's dress, and get it done quickly,' said Mr Deva. 'In fact, he's another client of mine and will be happy to do the work. You know,' he added thoughtfully as they crossed the wide hall and made ready to leave, 'you really could make use of this place in the school holidays and rent it out for formal dinners and banquets, as was done in the past. People could make their own catering arrangements with local firms, and it would all help to keep the place going. Many of us have known it over the years and would be happy to use it.'

They talked about this a little further before, after handshakes all round, the Deva family drove away in their car. Aunt Win pondered over it and later discussed it with her husband. 'I think it's a really good idea,' he enthused. 'It would make money and mean that the building was put to good use when it would otherwise lie empty. We might need a business manager. Do you think Mr Deva himself could help? He seems to have so many good connections. This is just the kind of link we need.'

He was right, and over the next few weeks this began the start of a new and more businesslike approach for the school. Meetings and conferences could be held there in the holidays, first on a small scale and then later on a full-time basis. The Drummonds would not have to do any of the catering, as outside firms were brought in, and a business contact of Mr Deva was to prove a competent and resourceful manager. As with so many other things about Four Winds, everything slowly fell into place.

Mr Deva also helped Aunt Win with the paperwork and formal arrangements now that Four Winds was clearly a school and needed to be registered as such. Aunt Win had already set in train the arrangements for regular inspections, so that the Government authorities could be satisfied that each girl was being taught according to the requirements of the National Curriculum. As a teacher who had long specialised in teaching children in their own homes, she was familiar with the regulations concerning this, but now needed to ensure that Four Winds' more structured status was properly arranged.

Meanwhile she had two other problems. The first was that of riding lessons.

'Yes, we'd be delighted to have girls from your school come along here,' said the manager of the riding school in the village. But then he named a price that Aunt Win knew was far beyond what most of the girls' parents could afford to pay. She looked gloomy. It wouldn't do to have just some of the better-off girls going riding while others could not.

'Why is it so terribly expensive?' she asked. 'Is it the staff that you have to pay? My girls would be happy to help with the cleaning and grooming of the horses they ride, I am sure.'

'No, it isn't really that,' said the manager, looking concerned and passing his hand across his forehead. 'It's the rent we have to pay for the field, actually. Land around here is expensive, and we need two big fields for all our horses. I'm renting another place, too, for jumps and so on. It all means I have to pass on the costs to people who come for riding lessons.'

Aunt Win thought for a while. 'We've got some spare land,' she said. 'I'd love it if we had horses and ponies there. Why not come, rent-free, and have them in our field? There's plenty of room, and areas for jumps and everything.'

It was soon settled. Within days, the horses were occupying their new home in a glorious meadow at the back of Four Winds. It meant that the girls could run out to greet them every day, and soon would know each one by name and learn how to call him. The riding lessons became a huge feature of school life, dominating conversations and forming something to look forward to and enjoy. Later on, there would be gymkhanas and competitions and wonderful events that would give the summer a magic of its own. Alison, in particular, felt that all this was a dream come true.

And Alison herself was the next thing for Aunt Win to think about. She was about to turn sixteen. She was four or five months older than both Gabriele and Elizabeth, the two nearest to her in age. Quiet and sensible, she had proved a calm and reliable influence in the school. Aunt Win had not forgotten the half-joking comment that she had made to her, in the very early days of term, that if pupil numbers increased, she would make her Head Girl. But was it fair to do that over the heads of Elizabeth – who had proved such a help with the computers – and Gabriele, herself a wise and thoughtful girl? In the end, Aunt Win decided to find out from the girls themselves. During the day, she found opportunities to chat with them in their various groupings, and without appearing to introduce the subject she discovered their views.

To her interest and slight amusement, she found that they seemed to consider Alison effectively Head Girl already.

'I think she is the senior among us,' said Gabriele. 'Why, it was Alison who first greeted me and showed me to my room. From the start I always think she is somehow the boss! It is true that she never makes herself important but, for me, I think it would be wise to give her – how do you say it? – the proper name, School Captain or something.'

Elizabeth was even more down to earth. 'Alison? Oh yeah, she's the reliable type,' she said. 'Old-fashioned and all that, but we get on pretty well now. I've always thought that if this was a normal school – with badges and all that – you'd make her Head Girl!' She looked at Aunt Win. 'Is that what you were planning to do? Oh, sorry,' she blushed and looked away. 'I shouldn't have asked. But if you want my opinion, I think it's a good idea.' A couple of weeks ago this would have been a sullen and even unpleasant remark, with a good deal of sourness behind it. But now it was said with simple common sense.

Aunt Win was also thinking of something else. Alison's parents wanted her to complete her education at a special music college in London. If all went well and she liked the idea, she would not stay at Four Winds right through to her 'A' level exams, as was normal. She would leave, to have the last two years of schooling in a place where classical music was the priority. This would mean that she had just a year and a half ahead of her at Four Winds. It would do her good to be given some responsibility during that time. And by the time she was due to leave, Elizabeth or Gabriele could take over as Head Girl.

She did not say any of this but gave Elizabeth an appraising look. 'If – and it's only an "if" at this stage,' she said, 'I decide to formalise things, I'd do it properly. It is true that Alison has a special role but there are a number of jobs to be done in an unusual place such as this, and we have a disproportionate number of younger girls and only three of you at the top end of the school.' She felt that if Alison were to be Head Girl she would need the support of a united team. Had Elizabeth yet thought out her own future in the school?

'I'd like you to think through – and talk over with your mother – your own future,' she said. 'You have been an enormous help, as I don't need to tell you, and it would be good to know that we could all rely on you for the future. The computers are all arranged now. It's your own work that matters. You're a bright girl and it is good having you here. Do you see yourself as having a long-term commitment to Four Winds? Don't let me know at once. Think about it. Come and tell me tomorrow or the next day.'

Elizabeth was rather taken aback by this. Somehow, without really thinking about it, she had allowed Four Winds to become part of her life: the walk through the village each morning, prayers in the schoolroom, a busy timetable with the work getting more and more interesting so there was no possibility of just dreaming or gazing out of the window, scrambling into pinafores – she had finally started to wear one and it had produced no comments – for work and talk and laughter in the kitchen, with favourite recipes being written up later into notebooks. Even life at home had changed. There were fewer rows, their mother seemed cheerful, and she and Joan seemed closer.

Now that the snow had gone, Elizabeth was having a long-planned visit into town this weekend to meet her friends. Yet somehow, the last three to four weeks had produced a gap that had been filled with new and different things. She thought about this. There had been more homework, and although she had initially resisted this she had found some of the lessons, especially history with Aunt Win's vivid descriptions of past events, and mathematics with Miss Crisp's amusing and practical approach, full of interest in spite of herself.

She had not liked being forbidden to bring teenage magazines into the school, and had told herself she was only doing this because Mum, as geography teacher, would be put in an embarrassing position if there was a public row. She had not, initially, liked the emphasis on music, although she had now got used to the frequent sound of the piano and to the singing lessons which were a break from academic work. She had felt superior over that silly affair of the younger girls and the matron and had shared in the general relief when it was over. But much else at Four Winds was, it had to be admitted, enjoyable. There were glorious grounds and sudden things like having a bonfire. The previous day they had all decided to have lunch as a barbecue out of doors, even though it was cold, and had cooked potatoes in the ashes and grilled sausages and mushrooms, because Uncle Harry had started a bonfire to clear away some garden rubbish and everyone agreed it was a pity to waste such a good fire. Was there any other school where teachers and pupils all cooked their own meals over an open fire out of doors in early February?

Elizabeth walked through the school grounds, thinking things through in the pale wintry sunshine, and acknowledged that she did feel part of this place. Would she feel differently once she'd met up again with her old friends? Should she wait and see?

Meanwhile, Aunt Win had also sounded out Alison, again without appearing to do so. She found her during the tea break, carefully working on a new kitchen rota to include Renu. She had already picked out two pinafores for the new girl and had pinned a note on the top one, with a friendly greeting signed by all the pupils welcoming her to the school.

'I thought it would be nice for her to find that on her first day,' she said. 'She actually showed us, this morning, where she'd like to sit. You know there's a space at the big table, next to Jeannie and just round from Marie. It's just waiting to be filled. And there's a spare shelf in the juniors' cupboard for her, too. Jeannie's promised to make out a label for her. As she's joining almost halfway through the term, we thought we ought to make her feel specially welcome.'

'You feel a real loyalty to Four Winds, don't you?' asked Aunt Win, stacking up some books and catching a pen that was in danger of rolling away.

'Oh yes, tremendously, I think we all do,' said Alison eagerly. 'Look at the way everyone's been helping Amanda. And I think the Hurry girls are fitting in well, which quite frankly didn't seem to be happening too well at first, although goodness knows we boarders tried. Oh, that reminds me, when does Amy become a boarder?'

'I've been thinking about that,' said Aunt Win slowly. 'I'm afraid I must ask you to make something of a sacrifice, Alison. Amy really needs to start boarding next week. Her parents are keen to get back to their own home and make plans for the move and so on.' She paused. She hadn't wanted to make the next suggestion but it was the only sensible one, given the arrangement of rooms in the house. 'Amy's been used to a room of her own, of course, and her own health makes it wise to continue that, at least for the time being. But I don't want her to feel cut off. The obvious solution would be to move her into your room, the annexe which adjoins Amanda and the twins. It would mean companionship and she'd have someone near if she was frightened in the night. But it does mean moving you. What would you say to that?'

'Oh, I, I hadn't thought of that,' said Alison, stopping what she was doing and putting her hands on her lap. She had a sudden mental picture of her own small and pretty room, which she had made attractive with some horsey posters and books and knick-knacks sent from home. She really didn't want to leave it. Amanda was her cousin; it was good to be sleeping near her. But Amy was small and frail and still rather scared. The poor kid needed a reasonable start at Four Winds. She grinned at Aunt Win and pulled her shoulders back. 'It makes sense, of course. It won't take me long to move. Where would I be going?'

'Well, it's nice of you to be so reasonable and thoughtful. There's a choice of other rooms, actually. With Renu coming, there'll be a general shuffling round. I wondered if you'd like to be nearer Gabriele? If we completely re-ordered that big bedroom, we could give each of you three older girls a private cubicle. In fact, the room divides into four quite logically. We could leave one cubicle free for storage. Would you like to come and have a look round it all with me? I'd value your opinion.' Privately, she was pleased at the way Alison had responded with maturity and common sense to the need to move. It was not only a load off her own mind – she had been drawing maps of rooms and shuffling names at intervals over the past two days to work out where Amy and, now, Renu would sleep – but it confirmed her in the thought that here was someone who was already acting as a thoughtful and responsible Head Girl.

While school life had its own busy pattern, Uncle Harry had been busy, mostly with trips to London and elsewhere, making final preparations for the Army expedition. A group of young officers were to arrive at Four Winds in a few days' time for a conference and it had been arranged that they would sleep over in his and Win's private part of the house, where extra beds had been moved into the two spare rooms. There would be talks and briefings, sorting of necessary equipment and a conference to ensure that all final questions were answered.

Next stop was Africa and the long-planned expedition. They were to help build roads and bridges to ensure better links with a port, paving the way for more prosperity and peace.

'It's all worked out really well,' Harry told Win that evening, sitting comfortably in what had become his favourite chair. 'We reach our final destination, assuming everything goes according to plan, just a few days before you finish things up here and the term ends. I'll be back for the end of term.'

He grinned across at her as she sat correcting some of the girls' English essays in the lamplight. 'I must say, this school business is all going ahead much more busily than we had ever imagined, isn't it? It's obvious that you'll be keeping it going at least for the next year. And you're still happy with it all?'

'I'm loving it,' said Aunt Win honestly. 'It's much, much more satisfying than just teaching a few girls English in Switzerland, although I used to enjoy that too. No, even with all the problems – making the computers work and that silly child stumbling downstairs – it's all been fun so far, and I do believe it's useful work and well worth doing.'

The government regulations and requirements for ensuring that the National Curriculum was being followed had proved less daunting than she had feared. If the school was to have a long-term future there would be regular and detailed inspections, and already all sorts of details such as fire drills and kitchen arrangements had been checked and proved satisfactory.

On the Friday Renu arrived – with an immaculately-sewn and very smart version of the school uniform complete with matching red blouses – and was shown enthusiastically round by the younger girls after being warmly welcomed by Alison. By now, morning inspection of rooms had been started, together with searching questions from Matron about hair-brushing and teeth-cleaning. As a result, a slightly scruffy air which had begun to pervade the school disappeared. People cleaned their shoes, arranged their things neatly, checked to ensure that there was never a toffee-paper or biscuit crumb anywhere, and generally took a pride in making Four Winds clean and comfortable.

Renu was quiet and careful in her work, but joined in a noisy hop-scotch game at break, and was happy to chat to the others over morning coffee and at tea-time, answering questions about her old school or hearing about plans for riding, First Aid, ballet, and skating.

'A doctor at the hospital told me Matron used to lead First Aid classes,' said Amanda importantly, sitting with her bandaged foot out in front of her, well protected by a stool so that no one would accidentally walk into it. 'So I asked her about it, and she said that once she's well settled in here, she might do some classes. Apparently, there's a certificate you

101

can earn, issued by the Red Cross or the St Johns Ambulance. I'd like to get one of those.' Already, in her mind's eye, she saw herself in a nurse's uniform, acting as a first-aider at local events, as she had seen others do at summer fetes and carnivals.

'Could we ask Mrs Ontwin if the classes could be held here?' suggested Alison 'There's plenty of space, and it would be nicer than the village hall. We could act as hosts. It could be on one weekday evening – shall I suggest it to her?'

There was general assent to this, even from Elizabeth, who had initially rolled her eyes at the idea and looked superior. First Aid seemed a very childish idea – it smacked of Girl Guides and people rushing about in a do-gooding way. But if these kids wanted it, she wasn't going to say anything.

'And there's ballet classes being discussed, too.' said Geraldine in an informed way. 'I know, because I saw Aunt Win with a copy of a notice from the village hall. Father Higgins brought it up. She'd asked him to find out about the times of lessons if he was passing – the hall's right next to his church – and now she's quite keen for all of us to go.'

'Will we all be doing this dancing?' asked Evangeline 'Me, I am happy about it. I like to dance, and I had lessons for some years. I have certificates at home from the dance academy.'

'Jeannie and I will certainly go. We did ballet when we were little, and then had to stop because it just couldn't be fitted in with school and everything. Now we can start again.'

'I too must do it – my parents ask this,' said Marie. 'I am not sure I like it. It is difficult, no? On the points of toes?'

'Not in a village ballet class,' said Jeannie, reassuringly. 'I think you can start at any level you like. Will there be exams and things we can pass?' She was still hoping that there would be more skating, too – there was a rink in the town – but ballet might be fun.

'The poster said there was a "fully accredited teacher,"' said Geraldine. 'I think that means she will get us doing exams and all that sort of stuff. It's exciting, isn't it?'

'Not so exciting as riding,' said Gabriele, with an instant nod and agreement from Alison. 'That reminds me Alison –

are you taking Mountjoy out tomorrow? Because I was thinking ... about this question of the cantering ... ' and the talk turned to horses and stayed there.

While the boarders were having this discussion round the fireside, Elizabeth was back at her home in the village, getting ready to go out. Joan – glued to an interesting television programme – was not listening to the talk, but their mother was trying to remind Elizabeth that she must be waiting for her at the agreed place when the evening ended.

'Now, you've got your money for pizza and coffee,' she said, 'and please don't go roaming round. Remember, just stay in the pizza-place where it's warm and cheerful, and enjoy a nice time with your friends. I'll collect you there at nine o'clock.'

It was a cold, wet evening, but Elizabeth was eager to be out. She had chosen her shortest skirt, black with a shiny belt, and a purple top with zigzag writing proclaiming the name of a really freakish pop group. She knew her mother didn't care for this outfit, but it would be good to be out of uniform, and she had a jacket slung over it as a gesture against the cold.

In the pizza-shop, the rest of the crowd were gathering. It was mostly girls – Elizabeth's old gang from school – and they greeted her with warmth.

'Hey – she's here! What's the news, then?'

'Marooned for the winter – did you finally dig your way out the village?'

'What's the new school like? D'you miss us?'

It was half-friendly, half-challenging banter. There was a lot of laughter, too – and soon they were sitting round, choosing pizzas while telling each other all that had happened since Christmas. After an initial awkward feeling – it seemed such a long time since they had all been together – Elizabeth felt that she was again among friends.

'Yeah, the new school's all right,' she found herself saying. She wasn't going to admit that she had hated it at first. 'Sort of small, though – and a lot of them come from abroad. The place used to be a sort of hotel! It still feels like one. Most of the girls live in there. It's kind of weird.'

'Sounds better than our old place,' moaned Shelley, who

103

had been more or less Elizabeth's friend at school, though they had often had rows. 'The headmaster's been a real loser this term – hasn't got a grip on anything. It's been really boring. When it was really cold we stuck around the place a bit, this week we got out – didn't we, Jackie? – and made off into town.'

Jackie, a short dark girl wearing, as most of them were, black with studs and earrings, nodded. 'Didn't come here, though,' she said, gesturing around the pizza place, 'not our scene in the daytime. They'd know we ought to be at school and go and report us, or something. We hung around the Square, as usual – and yeah, sure enough, the lads joined us.'

'Ron's changed, though,' said Shelley, taking up the story. 'He keeps saying we're boring. Got a load of really nice things for Christmas, and now he seems to think himself a lot older.'

'Is he still at school?' Elizabeth asked, 'I thought he was leaving at Christmas.'

'Yes, well, he was, but his family have a bit of money, you know … and he hasn't decided about working yet. His mum doesn't hassle him about things like that, so he dropped out of the training course he was meant to be doing. He sort of hangs around the school, meets us when we come out and that. Some of the younger lads – I mean, the ones in our crowd, but younger than him and still at school – feel he's somehow the leader now, and look up to him. Didn't happen like that before. Makes him seem, well, sort of special. I must say, I fancy him.'

A chorus of laughs and comments greeted this remark. Ron, although very good-looking, had often been regarded as something of a troublemaker. But an aura of glamour hung around him.

Later, when the boys joined them, Elizabeth found herself looking at Ron with new eyes. Yes, he did seem older. He had money to spare, too. This wasn't surprising, as he came from a wealthy family in the town and had always had more ready cash than most of the crowd. But now he had a certain swagger and poise. She found herself anxious to show him that she was more grown up, too.

'Been ages, hasn't it?' she remarked casually, after they'd

all made way for each other round the table, and ordered more coffee and drinks.

'Yeah – you look different.' His smile made her feel important, 'Is it a special college you're at then, this new place?'

'Well, sort of.' Elizabeth hedged. She wasn't going to tell him it was a small, friendly, rather old-fashioned school where her mother taught Geography. 'Yeah, and I help with the computers and things like that. It's more casual, not like a big ordinary school.'

He seemed uninterested in the details of school life, for which she was grateful. He might be impressed that they talked foreign languages at lunchtime, but then again he might not. And he certainly wouldn't want to know about helping to bake biscuits or singing round the piano.

'Got computers have they – it's that old hotel, isn't it? Must have quite a lot of that sort of equipment there.' He seemed really interested.

'Oh, yes – some really new stuff, just been updated. A Mr Deva came round the other day with new bits and pieces.' Elizabeth knew that the computers weren't really the very latest sort, but wanted to make it sound important. 'We've got a room specially set aside – you see, it's all very expensive.' She started to talk about it, running her fingers through her hair to make it stand up more, and lighting a cigarette to show how sophisticated she was. Shelley was looking jealous, while trying to show that she didn't mind. Elizabeth found her heart beating fast. She hadn't really ever had a boy – let alone Ron, more or less the leader of the others – take a special interest before.

'And some of the girls stay overnight – it's like a residential college?'

'Yes – that's right.' Put that way, it sounded quite adult. 'And it's quite different from school – sort of friendly and that.'

'No one locks them in at night!' he joked.

'Of course not. I mean – I'm not staying there, but it's all quite informal. They just sit round the fire and talk. Mrs Ontwin – she runs the school – and her husband have a flat of their own. Of course, there's other staff too.' She wasn't going to mention the word Matron, though a sudden image flitted across her mind of Mrs McMurdoch, who only that morning had sent her off at coffee-time to clean her nails and remove the black varnish she had been wearing on them. It brought her down to earth suddenly, so she was taken unaware by Ron's next question.

'I suppose the place is quite deserted then, at night-times, except for a few girls upstairs?'

'Yes – yes, I suppose so.' She hadn't really thought about it. Ron edged closer and took a sip of her coffee.

'Hey! Get lost! That's mine!' she joshed him playfully.

'Oh, sorry sister – didn't know you were that fussy!' It was fun having a stupid time with him. They were laughing and kidding with one another, and when the group started to break up, he was asking her to go out with him, take a walk round the town, see what was doing.

'No – honestly, I can't. I sort of promised my mum – I mean, it's miles to the village so she was going to give me a lift back,' she said.

'I could get you a lift. Go on, it's Friday! No college tomorrow' – he'd got it all fixed in his head that she was at a college now, rather than a school – 'It's the night for going out and about.'

'Oh, well, just once round the square then. Just a walk to get some fresh air.'

In the end, they went as a crowd. Shelley and Pauline screamed with laughter and got giddy running round and round the concrete seats in the shopping centre. Two of the boys slunk off to get warm in a shop doorway and smoke for a bit. Ron sidled up to Elizabeth.

'So – tell me more about this college place of yours,' he said, breathing rather heavily.

'Well – ' Elizabeth felt awkward, as there wasn't really much more to say, at least nothing she'd like to tell Ron 'It's – well – it's just where I'm studying, that's all.'

'And you're not staying there, then? No chance of meeting you there on Saturday night?'

'No – well, no of course not.' There had actually been plans for a meeting at Four Winds on Saturday evening, to discuss the First Aid class, but she had more or less decided not to go. Now she wondered if she might not change her mind. She could meet Ron there! Certainly her Mum wouldn't let her go off with Ron if he called at her house – she had never really liked him.

'You don't sound sure.'

'Well – actually, I could be there.'

'Meet me round the back then – no need to have to mix with all the other girls. I'd be shy.' He put on a baby face and made her laugh again. 'Is there a back entrance?'

'Yes – well, there's several. But they're all locked, at least, I think they are. We mostly use the front entrance. There's a patio round by the pool, and French windows there. But – well – I couldn't go near the pool ... oh, yes,' she suddenly remembered. 'There's a sort of side entrance, before you get to the kitchen door. It'll be locked, I think. Meet me outside there. You don't need to come into the building.' Already, she was fixing in her own mind what she would do. She would go to the First Aid meeting, sneak out by the front door and run round to meet him. It felt exciting, grown-up and dangerous.

Suddenly she looked at her watch. It was nearly nine o'clock. She broke free from him and led the way back to the pizza-shop.

'Half past eight tomorrow?' said Ron. 'Side entrance – agreed?'

'Yes – yes, I'll be there.'

Chapter 11

On Saturday evening Mrs Hurry was pleased to find that both girls were keen to go up to Four Winds for the First Aid meeting. As it wasn't a school day, of course they didn't need to wear uniforms. Elizabeth took a long time dressing. She kept discarding one outfit and planning another. Eventually, grumbling that she had 'nothing decent to wear', she hurried out wearing her favourite jeans and top, with a bomber jacket which was not really warm enough in this cold weather, but she thought it made her look older.

She had arranged to meet Ron at half-past eight, and the meeting began an hour earlier. Matron, relaxed and friendly as she had now settled into Four Winds and felt at home there, made them all laugh. She gave examples of people doing the wrong things for First Aid and causing hopeless muddles. Then she got serious for a moment, and explained how useful it would be for people to have a calm, independent knowledge of what to do in a real emergency.

'When Amanda and I were at the hospital the other day, someone was brought in who'd been scalded with hot water,' she said. 'Would you know what to do if that happened to someone? Would you know how to call an ambulance? And what to do before it arrived?'

She emphasised that what she was offering was only very basic advice.

'To be honest, the first rule always is "Call an ambulance". But things like artificial respiration – getting someone breathing again after they've been underwater – or stopping severe bleeding, are skills that every responsible person should know.'

The girls were interested and questions came fast.

'Will we get a chance to practise on real people, and are they painted with artificial blood or what? How do they act being hurt? Are they actors?' Everyone giggled when Jeannie asked this but she thought it a reasonable question.

'Well, obviously during the classes you just do the bandaging and so on with one another,' said Matron. 'But when you come to take your tests you'll find some people with horribly realistic injuries. There's an organisation that specialises in it – getting people dressed up to look as if they have broken legs and so on. There's plenty of artificial blood and mess.'

Elizabeth had become so interested in all this that she had honestly forgotten the time. At first she had been constantly looking at her watch, but as the questions developed, the thought of Ron waiting outside had gone further back in her mind. Now, suddenly, someone said 'What was that?' as there was a noise downstairs.

'It can't be Mrs Ontwin,' said Amanda and Renu both together.

'She and Major Ontwin are both out,' said Bernadette. They all knew this because they had called out cheerful farewells as they went out for an evening together, relaxing before the Army officers arrived next day.

'And it's not Mrs Drummond!' grinned Alison, as that good lady called out 'No, I'm here!' from further back in the room. She'd come to hear about First Aid and was keen to get her certificate. 'And it's not Mr Drummond either. He's out at the darts match at the pub.'

'It's nothing,' said someone else.

'No, listen!'

In a moment, Matron McMurdoch had leapt to the door, quickly followed by Alison and Gabriele. There was definitely a noise downstairs.

'Ooh, I'm scared!' said Marie, but Alison quickly said, 'Nonsense, everything's all right. We're all safe together.' And Amanda reached out to put her arm round Marie's shoulders. Small Amy went white. Renu found herself gripping the arm of her chair while Jeannie and Geraldine, as always in

109

moments of crisis, reached out for one another.

'Yes! There it is again!'

'I'm off downstairs,' said Mrs Drummond, pushing past everyone else to the door. 'No, don't try to follow me. I know every corner of this place. There's a telephone in the next room. Use it if you hear a shout. Just dial 9 and it will give you an outside line. Then call the police.'

The word 'police' made the atmosphere electric.

'You're not going down alone,' said Alison determinedly, and before Matron could stop her she had nipped past her and was with Mrs Drummond on the landing. They peered from behind a pillar and looked down between the bannisters. No one was in the hall, but there was a noise, a definite rasping noise and then a sudden crunch, from one of the downstairs rooms, as though someone had been cutting something, sawing away at something.

'It's from Aunt Win's office – no, from over there,' said Alison, straining to make her ears tell her the exact direction.

'That new computer room, that's it. But, look! Stand back!'

For down in the hall a figure suddenly appeared. He had run in from the kitchen area and was heading nimbly for the computer room. He called out hoarsely 'All clear!' as he opened that door. Alison, without further ado, made a sign to Mrs Drummond as if making a telephone call. Mrs Drummond nodded. Alison nipped back, put her head round the door of the schoolroom and hissed 'Telephone!' to Matron. Somehow, she felt if she shouted or even used the word 'Police' there would be panic and the intruders, whoever they were, would rush upstairs or start smashing things up or simply make a dash for it.

Matron, calm as always, kept the room completely still with one swift glance and was at the telephone in a moment. She dialled 9, then the emergency number 999, and within seconds heard the reassuring voice 'Emergency here. Fire, Police, or ambulance?'

'Police, please,' said Matron, glancing round to make sure that the door was closed. It was, and indeed several girls were leaning against it. Alison had urged them to do just this with a gesture before she tiptoed back to her own vantage-point on the landing.

110

'It's Four Winds here, the old hotel by the cross roads,' Matron calmly said. 'We've got intruders. I can't tell you more but hurry, please. I've got a roomful of children here upstairs, and two people watching on the landing. We've heard noises downstairs and someone is definitely breaking in.'

'Breaking in!' Suddenly Elizabeth's thoughts flew to Ron. It couldn't be him, could it? Had he got tired of waiting for her – it was past nine o'clock now – and forced his way in? Could he possibly have done anything so completely daft?

In a flash she realised she hardly knew him. He'd been 'one of the crowd', although richer and more exciting than most of them, and then suddenly last night he'd taken a real interest in her. But was he the kind of mad bloke who might break into a school to see someone?

'Yes, that's right, a noise downstairs. Yes, there's a whole crowd of us up here on the first floor. Downstairs – yes, it's lighted in the main hall but not elsewhere. No, I don't think we're burglar-alarmed. There is one but it's not switched on until everyone goes to bed and a final patrol is made of the building. Yes, I'll keep holding on. What? Already on its way? Even as we've been talking? Oh, what a relief.'

She was still holding on the telephone. Evidently the police wanted to keep the line open. The silence in the room was almost unbearable. Several of the younger girls, including Amy and Amanda, were in tears. Amanda was suddenly conscious of her bandaged foot. She felt so vulnerable. Suppose they all had to make a run for it?

Out on the landing, Alison and Mrs Drummond held their breath and watched as the first youth came staggering out of the computer room with one of the screens under his arm. Another followed, dumped a box of equipment in the hall and darted back for more.

'Thieves! They're stealing it.' Alison hardly mouthed the words but Mrs Drummond nodded. 'Did you ...?' she gestured the word for telephone. Alison nodded vigorously. Into her mind came a slogan she'd once seen on a poster: 'Don't have a go at the criminal. He may be armed!' But surely they just couldn't let these men get away with the school's computers? What else might they take? Was there money in Aunt Win's office? Suddenly with relief she remem-

111

bered that it was always locked when Aunt Win wasn't there. Oh, if only Major Ontwin was in the building! Or Mr Drummond, who was enjoying a pint down at the local pub. And why couldn't this have happened on Monday, when a great crowd of strong soldiers was due to arrive?

Nevertheless, and for all her fear, she continued to edge nearer the stairs, at first with a crazy thought in her mind of storming in and trying to stop the intruders.

The one in the computer room seemed to be having difficulties. He swore softly and there was a banging noise. Then it stopped suddenly, as if the person making it suddenly paused to see if anyone had heard him.

Mrs Drummond signed to her not to move further. She made a gesture of driving a car, meaning 'The police will soon be here.' They both craned forward and got a good look at both of the intruders as they staggered through the hall with another load of computer equipment.

'Not much, is there?' said one in a hoarse voice. 'I thought you said it was all the latest stuff. This is old. We won't get much for it.'

In spite of herself, Alison felt indignant. How dare they say Four Winds computers were old-fashioned!

Her next thought was, 'How will the police get in?' They couldn't break down the door. It was a huge one and the latch was strong. Before Mrs Drummond could stop her, she had seized the moment when the two men left the hall, nipped down the stairs and was at the door. She had opened it many times to visitors so there was no need to fiddle with anything, it was all second nature to her. The door swung open and she was on the outside of it. It was cold outside, and dark and frightening, but she was there for the police and they'd be along in a moment.

They were. Up the drive, in a blaze of headlights and purring engines but with no sirens, came two police cars, with uniformed men inside who leaped out and dashed forward.

'In here. This way!' A terrified Alison found her throat dry and her voice squeaky.

'Good girl. What's happened?'

Two policemen were already inside, and with a quivering

112

finger Alison pointed to the computer room. As she did so, one of the intruders came back into the hall and was caught red-handed. He roared out a filthy word and lashed out. A great commotion ensued. Upstairs, Mrs Drummond shrieked, shouts came from the schoolroom (they could hear that something was going on but Matron would not let them open the door) and Alison suddenly felt sick. The police were everywhere. Outside, two pursued a young man who was running down the drive.

'Is that the lot of you?' the police asked the young man in police custody in the hall. But he wouldn't say anything. 'Get me a lawyer,' he was saying. 'I'm innocent. I came here to meet a friend.'

Policemen leaped up the stairs. Mrs Drummond ran to them, explaining about the girls in the schoolroom, and they nodded and flew off in all directions to search every corner of the building. One knocked on the schoolroom door and called out 'Police. All's well!' and was finally let in after Matron had verified things over the telephone to the police station. 'Alison, where's Alison?' was her only cry as the door opened.

'If you mean the girl who opened the door to us, she's downstairs and perfectly all right, and probably enjoying herself,' grinned the policeman. 'There she was, cool as you like, outside the front door to let us in, showing us the way to where the thieves were operating. That's one smart girl you've got there. There's no need to cry, anyone. Just stay in here for a bit, though, while we clear the building. And we'll need to take statements.'

Alison was indeed beginning to enjoy herself. With a policeman taking it all down in a notebook, she described exactly what she had seen and heard. Gradually, the police reported from other parts of the building and the grounds. There was no sign of any other intruder. It looked as though the two who'd been caught were the only ones around, though neither would admit or say anything about this, giving no information of any kind.

Upstairs Elizabeth, shaken and white, was transfixed in her chair. Was it Ron?

It was. As they took his name and address, the whole story

became only too evident. It was all to come out in court later on. It was not Ron's first brush with the law. His chatting to Elizabeth the night before had only been to find out about computers or other valuable equipment at Four Winds. He had hoped to keep her talking while his chum got inside the building and they both managed to make off with computers or anything else they could steal, perhaps forcing Elizabeth to help them. Ruthless, bragging and cruel, Ron was still only a beginner at crime. He had no need to steal as he came from a well-off home, but his parents spoiled him and he had never been taught about right and wrong.

'A young lad marred in the making,' said a policeman, nodding sadly over it more than an hour later, after Ron and his friend had been led away. Everyone was slowly getting back to normal over mugs of tea.

'I've got to tell you. I know him,' Elizabeth had blurted out. 'I never thought he was a bad lot. He asked me to meet him here outside in the grounds but I got absorbed in the First Aid and it ran late. I never imagined he'd only come here to steal.' She was appalled at her own lack of judgement. How could she have let herself be used like that? Whatever would have happened if she had met him as they'd arranged? Later, lying in bed that night, she went over and over it in her mind. She desperately wanted to talk it all over with someone. But Joan was too young and she didn't want her Mum to know how nearly she'd been involved with Ron.

Back at Four Winds, the talk and excitement went on until a late hour. It was no use imposing a normal bedtime. When Aunt Win and Uncle Harry arrived they had to hear the whole tale. It would be in the local newspaper in due course! Alison found herself embarrassed to be so singled out for praise. When finally everyone went to bed, the younger girls needed extra comfort and reassurance. The burglar alarm was set and tested carefully and both Aunt Win and Matron went the rounds. Matron stayed with the younger girls until they dozed off. It was a night no one at Four Winds would ever forget.

Chapter 12

On Monday morning there was an air of something special at morning prayers. Everyone assembled as usual, with Elizabeth and Joan hurrying upstairs to the schoolroom after leaving their red berets and scarves on the pegs down in the front hall. The girls stood in their accustomed places, with Matron, Mrs Drummond, Miss Crisp and Mrs Hurry alongside. It was Gabriele's turn to choose a prayer and Scripture reading, and after she had read first in her own language and then in English, Aunt Win led everyone as usual in the Lord's Prayer. Then she made an important announcement.

'I think everyone has more or less been expecting this, but after the events of the weekend it seems especially appropriate,' she said. 'Alison, dear, would you step forward? As you know, most schools have a Head Girl. I think we know that we already have one, as Alison has taken on many extra tasks and responsibilities from the very first days here at Four Winds. Today I would like to make it official. With this little badge, I formally make Alison our Head Girl. It is not only a way of honouring her for her courage on Saturday night but of establishing her special leadership in the school. Alison, I know we can all rely on you to be loyal, cheerful and helpful in the year ahead.'

Everyone broke into warm and prolonged applause. Alison, blushing and hanging her head, at first did not know what to say. She gulped and accepted the badge from Aunt Win.

'As for Saturday night,' she said, 'that wasn't specially brave. I honestly didn't really think about what I was doing.

115

But ...' and here she held her head up because she felt that what she wanted to say was important, 'I know we are all very proud to belong to Four Winds, and I can't imagine a greater honour than being its Head Girl. I shall try to live up to it.' There was a further tremendous round of applause. From Renu and Amy, the newest girls in the school, to Amanda and the twins who had been there from the very beginning, there was loyalty and support for Alison. Four Winds was very proud of its Head Girl as she shyly pinned on her badge, a simple brooch depicting a rose, that matched the red velvet ribbons on the uniform.

After this, the morning's lessons seemed almost an anticlimax, but no one was ever allowed to slack at Four Winds and so work was soon under way. During the morning a policeman arrived to take further statements from various people about the events of Saturday night. Elizabeth, who had scarcely stopped thinking about what had happened and how deceived she had been by Ron, felt a renewed sense of embarrassment.

At lunchtime came a riding lesson for some of the girls, while the others went out into the grounds as usual. Sport was now playing a bigger part in the life of the school, and every new pupil meant that the possibilities were expanding. Netball had been started, using what had been the hotel's tennis courts. It was hoped to get together a good enough team to challenge some other schools in due course.

Soldiers who were due to go with Uncle Harry to Africa were having a meeting at Four Winds over the next few days, and part of the building was to be allocated for their use. It included the swimming-pool area and the nearby rooms, so would not affect the girls.

That afternoon, Alison and Aunt Win had a meeting to discuss various plans for the rest of the term, and Geraldine and Jeannie were on duty together for answering the door and helping to serve tea. They came downstairs to set out cups and plates on the table in the hall and found Uncle Harry busily talking to a young soldier. He was evidently giving him orders, as the soldier was writing things down in a notebook and saying things like 'Yes Sir' and 'Certainly Sir, that's very important'. Both girls tiptoed past so as not to disturb them, and then came back laden with trays and started to set out the tea-things as quietly as they could. The young solder looked up and seemed surprised to see them at work.

'Ah, these are my two young nieces,' said Uncle Harry, pausing for a moment from his lists and bits of paper. He gave the girls a friendly grin and called them over. 'Come and be introduced. This is Geraldine and this is Jeannie. This is Lieutenant Darrington, Andrew Darrington, who's part of the expedition to Africa. I'm making him work hard, as you can see. Is it teatime? We'd better get out and leave you girls to it. Wait here for a moment, would you, Darrington? I'll just round up those papers from upstairs and then we can get on and look at the vehicles outside.'

He bustled off and the two girls smiled shyly at Lieutenant Darrington, who evidently felt a bit awkward at being suddenly in their company.

'You seem to be working pretty hard. Have you got lots of people coming to tea?' he asked.

'Oh, it's only for all of us girls,' said Geraldine. 'We always have our tea down here, and today there's scones. We helped to make them.'

'You can have some, too,' added Jeannie eagerly. 'Mrs Drummond always sends a tea-tray up to Uncle Harry's room, I know. I could ask her to make sure there's enough for two.'

She was going to dart away but he stopped her. 'No, don't do that. I'm not sure what orders Major Battle has next for me. I'll probably have to hurry off somewhere. How many girls are there here, then? I didn't know Major and Mrs Battle had a big family.'

'Well, we're not all family!' Geraldine started to explain. 'Jeannie and me are Uncle Harry's nieces but the other girls aren't, of course. Oh ...' she broke off suddenly, 'we ought to finish setting out the tea-things. Would you mind if we went on doing that? Only it'll all get late if we don't hurry.'

'Of course.' He went with them to the table and, despite their insisting there was no need, he started to help them. Soon they were chatting like old friends and they were asking him about the trip to Africa.

'It will be quite an adventure,' he said. 'It's largely unexplored territory. There are bound to be some exciting moments. You might even get to hear about it on radio and television.'

'Is it really going to be dangerous?'

'Well, no, not really. It's mapping out the land, getting some bridges and roads under way – engineering work, essentially. But we're the advance party. You see, the idea is to help the people there, and it's a big team effort with their government and the British government. There should be some excitements. Part of the area is apparently held by some rebel forces. It all seems quite confusing. We've been warned to prepare for any eventuality.'

'Do you mean being captured or something like that?' The words were hardly out of Jeannie's mouth before she felt silly for having said them. It sounded as if she was just an ignorant schoolgirl who didn't know that things like that didn't happen outside adventure stories. But he gave her a cheery grin.

'Oh, I don't think we're likely to be captured or tortured. Incidentally, your uncle is an excellent commanding officer and we're all very glad to be under his leadership. No, but I suppose there's always a risk. I tell you what, if anything ghastly happens to us, I'll send you a special code-word! I'll do it by a radio message and you can know that you must get in touch with the Ministry of Defence in London and arrange for help to be sent to us.'

'What sort of code-word?' both girls asked together, and then laughed because they had both said the same thing at once.

'Well, er ...' he looked around him. 'Well, what's the name of this house? Four Winds, isn't it? Very well then, I'll send a message to say "Tell the Four Winds we need help." Is that a deal?'

'That's a deal,' they said and, in Four Winds style, held out their hands for him to shake on it. Looking slightly surprised, he did so. They went on setting out the tea-things and just as they were finishing, the door of Aunt Win's office opened and Alison came out.

'Hallo, twins!' she said cheerily, and then smiled at the

visitor. Jeannie and Geraldine introduced him. He held out his hand to shake hers but seemed puzzled.

'Are you another niece?' he said. 'Major Battle didn't tell me he had such a large family.' He was obviously also baffled by the fact that all three girls were dressed alike.

'It isn't a family,' said Geraldine, giggling slightly at the thought. 'It's a school. Didn't you know that Aunt Win – Uncle Harry's wife – is our headmistress? This is Four Winds School and Alison's our Head Girl!'

Alison blushed and looked at the floor. 'Don't be silly, Geraldine,' she said. 'I'm sure Lieutenant Darrington doesn't want to know that.'

'She was just appointed this morning,' explained Jeannie.

'Jeannie, please! You're being embarrassing. Goodness, there's the bell. You'd better hurry and get the rest of the tea-things. I'm going up to collect my geography notes. Er, goodbye, Mr … er …' She had forgotten his name despite having used it only moments before.

'Darrington,' he filled in for her. 'And please don't be embarrassed. I think it's splendid that you're the Head Girl! I just didn't know this was a school. All that we soldiers were told was that Major Battle would be holding the Orders Group at this house in the country! We're going to be here – a dozen or so of us – over the next few days.'

'Yes, Mrs Ontwin told us, a whole bunch of soldiers invading our school! But you're going to be using the back part of the building – it's out of bounds to us – so we won't get in your way or anything.'

'And Major Battle will be keeping us pretty busy, I can tell you! Maps and plans and lectures and notes and preparations. I've already got a stack of work to do. Er, do satisfy my curiosity. Can I just ask something?' Alison looked very pretty standing there, clutching her books and with her blue-grey uniform dress bringing out the colour of her eyes. He wanted to satisfy his curiosity about something but also enjoyed talking to this polite and shy girl. 'Why do you call your head-mistress Mrs Ontwin? Isn't her name Mrs Battle?'

Alison smiled, her shyness receding. She glanced briefly in the direction of Aunt Win's office. 'It's quite simply really,' she said, 'but I'm lowering my voice because it's something

119

we sometimes laugh about. You see, her Christian name's Winifred, usually shortened to Win. So you can just imagine, being a headmistress with a name like Mrs Win Battle!'

They laughed together. 'So you see,' she went on, 'as Jeannie and Geraldine call her Aunt Win, the rest of us started calling her Mrs Ontwin and, well, the name stuck. It's even on the official school notices now. Look, I really must get my geography notes upstairs. In a moment a whole bunch of girls will come thundering down here, all demanding tea. Where did Major Ontwin go? Shouldn't you be with him?'

'Yes. He told me to wait here but perhaps I'd better ...' At that moment, Uncle Harry reappeared on the landing.

'Darrington! Sorry to keep you waiting. Here, catch this.' he tossed down a map case. 'Meet you outside. I'll need the main vehicle round at the back. Drive it round, would you, and meet me there? Follow the driveway. Hello Alison! Hope this hasn't held up the school tea. We'll be well out of your way from now on.'

'Yes Sir.' Andrew Darrington deftly caught the neat bundle of papers that had been tossed down to him, then grabbed his cap, shook hands briefly with Alison with a nice smile and hurried off. At the front door he paused to put on his cap and salute.

'Goodbye, Head Girl,' he said. 'Wish us luck in Africa! Tell the twins I enjoyed meeting them.' And with a shy grin he was gone. At that moment the bell went and a stream of girls headed down the stairs, sweeping up Alison among them. She hurried on to put away her books and then rejoin the others, and found that for the rest of the afternoon the image of a good-looking young soldier, with a nice smile and polite manners, kept coming between her and the work she was meant to be doing. It was the first time anyone had ever saluted her.

Chapter 13

During the three days of the Army conference, no one in the school saw anything of the Army team. The girls knew that they must not in any way disturb the conference that was taking place, or do anything that would put at risk the important preparations for the expedition. In any case, the soldiers were using a part of the school that was strictly out of bounds. The girls did hear, occasionally, noisy arrivals and departures of vehicles and the sound of orders being shouted or of busy feet running back and forth outside. They sometimes heard loud masculine laughter late at night, and once there was some noisy and cheerful singing of 'For he's a jolly good fellow!' That was obviously the end of the conference, because next morning they heard all the Land Rovers and other vehicles driving away. At lunchtime Major Ontwin popped his head round the door of the dining-room to talk to Aunt Win, and he seemed cheerful and satisfied.

'All gone,' he reported. 'It was a good conference, and we're a united team and raring to go. Next stop Africa!' He grinned round at all the girls. 'Come and give us a good send-off when we make our grand departure in a couple of days' time,' he said.

They certainly did. Some Army vehicles arrived a few days later and soldiers leaped down from them to help Uncle Harry load up. Alison looked to see if Lieutenant Darrington was among them. He was, but they were all much too busy to notice the schoolgirls. It was the morning coffee-break when Uncle Harry finally checked the vehicles and swung himself up into one of them. The girls were gathered and rushed out of the front door to wave the team off. Uncle Harry blew Aunt Win a kiss, then gave a big thumbs-up sign to all the girls, who responded with a resounding cheer. The soldiers cheered back and there was a lot of waving and calling out of 'Good luck!' and 'Come home safely!' To continued cheers, the team of vehicles made its way down the drive and out through the gates on to the main road.

Aunt Win evidently wasn't going to allow herself to mope. It was a day for speaking French at lunch, so everyone tried their best to think of things to say in that language about Africa, the expedition, and wishing all the team a safe journey. The rest of the day included a ballet class for all the younger girls, except for Amanda who had of course to stay behind and would not be able to take up the classes until her foot healed.

They found themselves divided into two groups in the village hall, where classes of a high standard were being taught. By now they had all obtained ballet shoes and leotards. If any of them imagined that the classes would just be a chance to lark about, they were wrong. It was serious and enjoyable work, beginning with *pliés* at the barre and going on to centre-floor work. Jeannie found that it was easy to pick up again her memories from earlier lessons when she had been younger. She found that she loved the clear rhythm of the music telling her what to do, the ballet teacher's voice saying 'And one and two and three and four. See if you can raise that arm a little higher, like this.' Back at school, after supper, she and some others begged Alison to play the piano so that they could practise some of what they had learned that day. Jeannie liked the deep sweeping curtsey with which each ballet lesson began and ended, the satisfying French names for clear-cut movements, the sense of swift and graceful actions bringing the music to life.

It was a very windy, bitterly cold evening. Since the thaw the weather had been reasonably mild, but in the last few days it had got colder again. The girls had hurried back from the village in a crocodile led by Miss Crisp, who had gone down to fetch them after their lesson. She had urged them on because of the cold, but no urging was necessary. The big house was cosy and welcoming. The evening in the pleasant music-room had blotted out the mounting gale outside. When Alison finally called a halt and put her music away, Evangeline and Marie volunteered to run down to the kitchen and ask for jugs of apple-juice as everyone was warm and thirsty after the dancing.

'Ballet is going to replace skating as the thing you love best,' said Geraldine to Jeannie as they were changing out of their ballet clothes for the second time that day.

'Mmm, could be. I wonder if I could get some more books on ballet from the library? All our old ones are packed away. I suppose they're in the storage place in Cornwall. I do like Madame Lejeune, don't you?' The ballet mistress had a French name and had studied for a while both in Paris and in Russia.

'Yes, and I like the walk down to the village and being able to go to the sweetshop afterwards and buy things! Do you ever feel, Jeannie, just a little bit enclosed here? It's very different from being day-girls at ...' But here she got suddenly cut off and ended her sentence with a shriek because suddenly all the lights went out!

'What's going on?'

'Help! It's all dark!'

'I can't see anything!'

There were a few moments of chaos before Aunt Win's clear voice rang out. 'It's all right everyone, it's just a power cut!' She went from room to room with a torch. 'Come on downstairs so we can all be together. We've got plenty of candles, and we'll sit in the kitchen. No need to be scared, Amy. Come on, Marie. Is everyone accounted for?'

Slowly, with much stumbling and giggling, they gathered together in the dark. Geraldine and Jeannie gave special help to Amanda, who was fumbling with her crutches. Carefully they got her downstairs. The glowing logs in the fireplace in the hall gave the whole place an eerie look. It felt exciting but mysterious and weird. The kitchen was lit with candles and there were glasses of apple-juice on the table. It looked cosy and inviting. Soon everyone was sitting round the table or perched on nearby chairs, swapping stories and wondering how the power-cut had happened and how long the lights would be off.

123

'Are you sure it's a power-cut, not just a fuse that needs changing?' Alison asked Aunt Win. 'Yes, I've checked,' said her headmistress. 'It's annoying as we just don't know how long it will last.'

'It's the wind, that howling gale outside,' said Matron, who had been going round checking that everyone was all right. 'I think the power-lines must be down. If you look out of the windows all you can see is blackness, so obviously this whole district must have lost its electricity. We're on a breezy hill here at the best of times. No wonder this house is called Four Winds! But tonight – just listen! – we might as well be in a storm at sea!'

They did listen and it was ferocious. Rain began to lash against the windows. 'It's so cold! It might turn to snow again,' somebody speculated.

'Good!' said several voices. The snowy weather had been enjoyable. Meanwhile it was fun to be all together in the cosy kitchen, with a sense of drawing together against the dangers outside.

'Let's sing,' said Aunt Win. 'Let me hear that song you've all been practising at your singing lessons. Do you think you'll have it ready for the end-of-term concert?'

'Which song?' asked the twins and some others together. 'We've been learning three or four!'

'Let's start with the German one and then do that nice "Nymphs and shepherds", suggested Amanda.

And so, after a few false starts and some initial giggling, they got singing. The lovely music caught them up and swept away the fears of the younger ones. They sang all the songs they had been learning in their singing lessons. Some went better than others but Aunt Win pronounced herself delighted. Then she called for other contributions and produced one herself, with a lively round which meant dividing everyone into parts. They learned quickly. Soon it was going well but ended in laughter when one group finally got it wrong and they all collapsed into a tuneless muddle! They sang it again and again, satisfied when they finally got it right. Then Mrs Drummond, not to be outdone, got them doing a silly action-song of 'Heads, shooulders, kness and toes' and Mr Drummond, a lone male voice, started up 'Cockles and mussels' and they all joined in that, too. Then came a pause while no one could think of anything else for a while, followed by a sudden rush of ideas as people produced songs they'd learnt at other schools, pop songs, family favourites and songs with clapping or stamping of feet.

Eventually Matron looked at her watch and said something to Aunt Win. It was bedtime for the younger ones.

'We'll all go up together,' she announced. 'Anyone holding a torch, take hands with someone who isn't. I'm leading the way with a candle.' It was exciting. The whole house felt different in the dark. Someone let out a wild moaning sound but Matron cut her short. 'Who was that? We're not going to have any silly games, please.'

'Sorry Matron,' came Evangeline's voice. She had been pretending to be a ghost but it was true that small Amy, gripping Geraldine's hand, was quite scared enough already and several of the girls were decidedly more jittery than they were prepared to admit.

Together, with Matron leading and Aunt Win bringing up the rear, they made their way down the kitchen corridor and out to the main hall. Here Matron stopped again and said crossly, 'Evangeline, you have been told once. You are not to make that silly noise. Now, I'm being serious.'

'But no, Matron, I did not, truly not!' Evangeline's voice was indignant, her accent stronger than usual in her anxiety to clear her name. Alison turned the beam of her torch so that she could see her face. If someone was misbehaving and deliberately trying to make people scared, the Head Girl would back up Matron in getting it stopped.

'Honestly Matron, she didn't!' affirmed Amanda who was just behind. 'It must have been something else.'

'There it is again!' They all heard a distinct, low moaning sound.

'Ooh! Not more intruders!' There were screams of terror now and a real sense of panic. 'Nonsense, everyone! It's probably just the wind.' Matron's voice did not wobble, though deep inside herself she did feel fear. 'Come along. We're all going up to bed and not making any silly fuss just because the wind howls in a storm.'

'Perhaps we might sing again,' Alison was starting to

suggest, when a noise really did startle them, though it was something which in the ordinary way would not cause fear. Somebody knocked at the front door.

The sound made them jump out of their skins. They clutched each other and everyone started talking at once: 'Who can that be?' 'At this time of night?' 'Who'd be out in this weather?'

'It's a perfectly reasonable time of night,' came Aunt Win's voice calmly. 'It only feels late because of the power-cut. It's just someone who has come to call. We don't often get evening visitors but there's no reason why we shouldn't. Just wait here. Gather round the fireplace. Stick an extra log or two on the fire, would you Alison, while you're about it?'

She deliberately kept her voice steady, but memories of the weekend burglary were all too close. Could it possible be happening again? She felt suddenly glad that Mr Drummond, this time, was in the building, downstairs in the kitchen where they had all been singing. He would come at once if he were needed. While she was thinking this, she advanced to the front door where the knocking had now become urgent.

'Good evening,' she said loudly as she opened the door. But no one answered her. Instead a shivering girl stood there, holding a coat around her and weeping bitterly. At the sight of the crowded room, the glowing fire and Aunt Win holding a torch, she rushed forward. She tripped and fell. Everyone ran towards her but Renu got there first. She flung her arms around the figure on the doormat.

'Meena!' she screamed. 'It's my sister Meena!'

There was a confused babble of voices as Aunt Win shut the front door and Matron called for everyone to stand back so the girl could get some air, while people waved torches about and shouted to one another. Eventually Matron raised the girl up and half walked, half-carried her to the fireside.

'Renu, I couldn't bear it, I had to run away!' the girl sobbed. 'I got your letters. I just took my ticket and passport and ran off. I thought I'd get to your school in England. Oh, I'm so glad I've found you!'

Gradually, between gulps and sobs, the story came out. Meena had not been happy at her school in India and Renu's letters made her long to join her at Four Winds. She made a

126

sudden decision to run away. She had left a note for her grandparents, with whom she'd been staying in India, and hurried to the airport, catching the first plane to England.

'I told the airline I wanted to change my ticket for an earlier date and they just agreed and stamped it. Sitting on the plane it all felt so exciting. But I'm tired, I'm frightened, I'm cold!'

'And your parents must be terrified!' said Aunt Win. 'The first thing your grandparents must have done was to telephone them. They will be out of their minds with worry. They've probably had the police of two countries searching for you. We must call them at once, before we do anything else. Yes, Matron, she needs a hot drink and let's get her out of that wet coat and wrap her in a blanket or something.'

In moments she was in her office and dialling the Deva family's number. The school could not hear what she said but she soon called for Meena to come across. By the light of a torch, Meena poured out her story to her parents through her tears. Aunt Win, after setting up the torch on a table, closed the door to give her some privacy. Eventually, tear-stained and still hiccupping, Meena re-opened the door and called 'Mrs, er, Headmistress! My father says he would like to speak to you again, please.'

'We're so relieved our daughter is safe!' came Mr Deva's voice down the line. Normally a steady and dignified man, he was close to tears. 'You can't imagine what the last few hours have been like! Just to hear her voice and to know she is all right! It's almost crazy what she has done.' He filled in the gaps in Meena's story: 'It was some time before her grandparents discovered the note and realised she had not gone as usual to school that morning. By the time the alarm was raised she was already halfway across the skies, but she hadn't made clear what she was doing so it took a while before we thought of checking the airlines. I want to come and get her right away, of course, but she said something about a power black-out there?'

'Yes, we've got a power-cut, no electricity because of the storm,' said Aunt Win. 'It might be dangerous to set out in this weather, and there are no street-lights or any kind of guidance to get you up to the house. Of course, you must

127

make your own decision, but if you feel it's best to wait and collect her in daylight tomorrow morning, you can be sure we will take good care of her for the night.'

They talked further. The wind and storm still howled. It was obviously crazy to drive out in such weather. Finally it was decided that Meena should be put to bed at Four Winds and her parents would come and fetch her as soon as morning arrived.

'I had some money I'd been keeping, and thought it would be enough for a taxi from the airport, but it wasn't,' Meena told the girls round the fireplace. 'Eventually I just told the driver to set me down at a nearby village and I walked and walked along the main road. I didn't have a torch or anything but Renu had given me the school's address and I just kept on walking, and asked once at a petrol-station and again when someone offered me a lift. I didn't accept the lift but he did point me the right way. It wasn't far by then. What terrified me was everything being so dark. I couldn't understand why there wasn't a single light anywhere, except faint glows from behind people's windows.'

She was speaking excitedly now that she was warm, but the journey and the cold had obviously done her no good. Her body desperately needed rest. Matron had already re-organised sleeping arrangements so that Meena could share with Renu for the night. She now bustled all the girls upstairs, making sure they still held hands and shared torches. Rules about cleaning teeth and washing properly were still to be strictly observed, she reminded them, and no one was to start getting silly or over-excited.

Soon Meena was tucked into bed in a borrowed nightgown. Matron gave her a warm drink and an aspirin as she had a headache and was shivery. Renu was told that they must not lie and talk for hours, though they were allowed to chat as she made ready for bed. Soon there was calm over all the younger girls' rooms. Talking was only allowed for five minutes after lights-out, and then Matron made her rounds and a silence descended. She made sure that torches were placed by the doors of each room for any night emergency. She twitched a pillow back into place here, tidied away a fallen garment there, and finally made her way downstairs to where Aunt Win

128

was sitting with Alison and Gabriele by the fire.

'Well, we won't talk of it any more tonight but please remember, she is not to be treated as a heroine in the morning,' Aunt Win was saying. 'She must stay in bed and rest, and get up when her parents come. No one must go in and talk to her; she will need a lot of sleep. Her room is strictly out of bounds to everyone except her sister. Of course we are all pleased that she is safe and well. We must just hope she has not caught a dreadful chill by being out in this storm. But she has done a very wrong and foolish thing in running away from her school in India, and so terrifying her parents and grandparents, and I don't want any of you to think otherwise.'

'Will she stay here as a pupil, though Mrs Ontwin?' asked Alison, thinking that this was a reasonable question, even though Meena's arrival had been so exciting and strange.

'That's for her parents to decide,' said Aunt Win coolly. 'It's not something I'm going to discuss now, not even with my Head Girl! It's time you two older girls were in bed now. Yes, I know it's early, but it's been a crazy day and I'd just as soon have you all safely upstairs and know where each of you is for the next few hours. Being a headmistress of a school full of young girls can be a very worrying business!'

Chapter 14

The Deva parents arrived the next morning and had a tearful reunion with Meena. She went home with them in the family car, well wrapped up in blankets against the cold. She was feverish and unwell after the long walk in the storm following the flight from India, and would need several days to rest and get well. Then they would decide what to do for the future.

Meanwhile, half-term was drawing near. The school would close for several days. All the girls who were not going to their own homes would be staying with those who were. Jeannie and Geraldine would be going to Grandma's. Already she had planned some treats and outings. Much as they loved Four Winds, it would be good to take a break from school.

Gabriele was flying home to Austria. 'It means I can see my own beloved horses again – and my brothers and sisters too,' she added as an afterthought.

'Have you got lots of brothers and sisters?' asked Alison rather enviously. Being an only child, she was often rather lonely at home, much as she loved her parents and enjoyed their company.

'Yes, there are six of us. Actually, I am very fond of them all. Franz is the closest to me in age. He's seventeen and has been studying in Salzburg but is due to come and do some work in England soon. Maria is already married with a home of her own. I was her bridesmaid last year at her wedding. Her husband, Joseph, is a publisher and they live not far from us. And then there are the three younger ones, Isabel, Vroni – that's Veronica – and Maximillian. I suppose we are a big family, certainly a happy one!'

'There are five of us,' piped up Jeannie, thinking of her three little brothers in Japan. 'We're a happy family too.' Suddenly, the boys and her parents seemed very far away. Geraldine put her arm round her and gave her a squeeze. 'We'll be seeing them all at Easter,' she said. 'Daddy always organises an Easter-egg hunt. He'll do it this year, the same as always, and we'll be with him to enjoy it, either at Grandma's or in Japan.'

Before the school closed for half-term, Aunt Win organised a special meeting.

'There are certain administrative matters that we need to sort out before we all take our break,' she said. 'First, you need to know that Meena will be joining us as a pupil after half-term!' There was a round of applause at this. They all knew that Meena had been wrong to run away from school in India but they all admired her courage and sense of adventure. It would be good to have her in the school. Alison, Gabriele and Elizabeth were particularly pleased because she was their age and would alter the balance of numbers slightly in favour of the older girls. Renu, who had already suspected that her sister would be joining her at Four Winds, beamed with pride and pleasure. They would spend half-term talking about it, and she would love showing her older sister around the school and helping to settle her in.

'Second, I am interviewing another girl today who might be joining us. She lives locally but I understand the plan is for her to be a boarder here,' went on Aunt Win, glancing down at her notes. 'She too is fourteen coming up to fifteen, and so will be in the senior class here. There's another slight change, too, that Elizabeth and Joan may already have mentioned to the rest of you. As lessons and other activities have expanded, Mrs Hurry has kindly agreed to be on duty here three nights a week, so for those nights – Tuesday, Wednesday and Thursday – Elizabeth and Joan will of course stay here, too. That makes them, I suppose, semi-boarders!' This called for another round of applause, led by Alison. She wanted the Hurry girls to know that they were a valued and important part of the school. Both seemed quite happy at the prospect of joining the boarders for part of the time, and Joan was positively beaming.

'Now, I'd just like to say that so far I've been very proud of you all here at Four Winds,' concluded Aunt Win, putting down her papers and looking round seriously at them all to gather their attention. 'As you know, I never really planned to start a school. It's really been a sort of experiment! So there's just one more thing to say, and it's this. Of course I have made plans for the summer term – I've had to – but the whole future is still very much up in the air. The next few weeks will be crucial. Whether or not Four Winds has a future as a school really depends on whether or not we can make a success of it in this next half-term. If things don't go well, I shall have to give it all up and inform your parents that they must make fresh plans for your education. It wouldn't be fair on them or on you to be running a school that had no real future. So it's up to all of us. I'd like you to think a bit about that over half term.'

There was silence after this speech, while everyone recognised the seriousness of what she had said

'Don't be gloomy,' said Aunt Win. 'It's all been going well so far, and you're a great team! You must all enjoy your half-term break, and then we've got so many things to enjoy as the spring weather comes and all our plans for First Aid classes and the concert and so on. Now perhaps we'll end on a happy note. Alison, if we all went into the music room, do you think you could play so that we could all join together in some singing to round off this half-term?'

Half-term came and went, an enjoyable break for everyone. At Grandma's, Jeannie and Geraldine found themselves relishing the peace and the feeling of just being themselves. Grandma was quite happy to hear endless stories of school life and to ask questions and give her views as she rolled pastry or made them buttered toast. Her little house was spick-and-span and its garden was beginning to show signs of life. Spring was on its way. In the evenings she read them stories as their mother had done since they were small, and one night they sat up late talking about how things had been when she herself was a girl, long ago during the Second World War.

When they got back to Four Winds the day half-term ended, there was a glad reunion for everyone. Chattering, laughing, swinging suitcases up the staircase and hurrying to unpack things into familiar rooms, the girls filled the house with a cheerful din. Aunt Win had spent part of half-term visiting friends. Mr and Mrs Drummond had taken a much-needed break and Four Winds had been quiet. Now it had come to life again. Aunt Win was cheerful. There had been a long newsy letter from Uncle Harry. All was going very well indeed in Africa. She herself was feeling rested and well. Her mood was reflected in that of all her pupils.

Elizabeth and Joan arrived too, even though there were no lessons until the next morning. They were to be shown the rooms where they would sleep when they were boarding for part of each week. There had been a further re-organisation of bedrooms, which were now firmly divided into 'Lower School' for the younger girls along one corridor and 'Upper School' for the older girls along another. The names stuck and soon everyone was using them.

Hurrying down into the hall to collect a further suitcase, Elizabeth got a tremendous shock. Standing there, looking rather shy and wearing the Four Winds uniform complete with red beret, was Shelley!

'Hey!' Elizabeth couldn't help herself. 'What on earth are you doing here?'

'Doing here? I'm coming here to school!' said Shelley. 'I tried to ring you over half-term to tell you but never got any reply.'

'Yes that's right, we were away. We were staying with some friends of Mum, but whatever made you come to Four Winds?' She was utterly amazed. Shelley belonged to a completely different part of her life. She had not had any contact with her since that evening at the pizza-shop.

Shelley looked around as if to make sure no one was listening.

'It was my Gran,' she said, 'after all that trouble with Ron. You know his case comes up in court soon? They say he'll probably be sent away for years and have a criminal record all his life, that will follow him wherever he goes.'

Elizabeth nodded. Thoughts about Ron and the burglary had never really gone from her mind. She kept wondering what would have happened if she'd kept her promise to meet him, and whether he would have involved her in trying to steal the computers. Even now a shudder went over her when she thought about it.

'Well, my Gran was hopping made when she heard about it,' said Shelley. 'Of course, it was all over the town in no time. His parents keep saying the police were just picking on him but everyone knows that's not true. My Gran knew he was a friend of mine and she came round and talked to my mum about it. She said she knew I was getting in with what she called a bad crowd. There was an awful row at home, I can tell you. They shouted at one another. I kept well out of it.' She stopped and looked at Elizabeth. 'You know things haven't been right at home for ages, since Mum and Dad got divorced.' Elizabeth nodded sympathetically. All the time that she and Shelley had been at school together over the previous two years, she had known that the girl had been having a difficult time at home. 'Well, my Mum had kept saying she wanted more of a life for herself and all that. She used to go out a lot. And I didn't really like her new boyfriend, Bill. I really wished she'd let Dad come home. I knew he wanted to. It was all a mess.' Shelley took a deep breath and was quiet for a moment. Then she went on. 'Well, my Gran suddenly announced she thought I ought to get away from our old school and make a fresh start. Get into a better crowd, she said. She'd put up the money and I was to go away to a boarding school. Boarding school! I can tell you, I really created a row about that. How dare she try to send me away! But Mum backed her up. She said that she knew I'd been skipping school and wasting time in the town and all that.' Shelley looked at the floor and traced a pattern with her toe.

'Actually, I knew Gran was being really good. She has a bit of money and she likes to go abroad on coach trips with her friends and have holidays, but here she was offering to spend it on school fees for me instead. I've always got on well with her but I haven't seen so much of her lately, somehow. I never felt comfortable with her because she'd ask me about school and all my friends and that. Well, when I saw that she was serious about this boarding school thing, I knew I couldn't really fight it so I finally agreed. But then I had a sudden thought that you were at school here. And I said couldn't I go to Four Winds. And, well, I had an interview here just before half term and here I am!'

So this was the new girl Aunt Win had mentioned at that last meeting, just before the school had broken for half-term! Shelley Willmot, standing there in a grey-blue uniform and with a suitcase waiting beside her, looked shy and uncertain and rather out of place.

'My Gran dropped me off here but I didn't want her to stay,' she said. 'I suddenly felt I'd rather face it alone. And then I hoped you'd be here.'

'Well, I am,' said Elizabeth. She looked Shelley up and down. Suddenly she felt a seriousness inside herself. The hot, uncomfortable feeling that she had whenever she remembered Ron and the burglary melted slowly away. In its place came a new sense of purpose. She looked down at her own grey-blue uniform and felt very much a Four Winds girl. With a sudden grin she held out her hand. She and Shelley had never shaken hands before, but it was a Four Winds tradition.

'Welcome to Four Winds,' she said. 'You'll enjoy it here. It's sort of mad, in a way. Last half-term we had a power-cut, a girl running away to us from India, the burglary and a whole lot of soldiers using this place as a training ground! We're made to speak foreign languages at meal-times – oh, don't look so scared, there are ways of surviving! – and we're starting First Aid classes. And I haven't even told you about doing the cooking.' She seized Shelley's suitcase and started up the stairs. 'Come on, I'll find out from Alison – she's the Head Girl – where your room is. You might even be sharing with me. I'm a part-time boarder now too. Let's go and find out.'

Chapter 15

There was plenty to talk about as the school organised itself for the second half of term. Meena and Renu were keen to start a new chapter of life as sisters together in the same school. Proudly, Renu showed Meena around everywhere and instructed her in the school traditions. Privately, Meena smiled at this. As the older girl she had always taken the lead in everything before. It was amusing to see her younger sister so confidently in charge! But she also knew that she was going to have to work hard to prove herself to her parents and to the rest of the family. Running away from school in India had been a silly and wrong thing to do but she had felt desperate and lonely. Now her parents had listened to her and were prepared to let her attend the school that she had struggled to reach that stormy night. She simply must make a success of it!

Gabriele talked about her family and the good time she had had during the holidays. There had been riding and picnics and an expedition to the mountains. She talked about her brother Franz and the fun they had had together. In fact, it was evident that she had not really wanted to return to school.

Alison, on the other hand, although she had loved being at home, had returned to Four Winds with renewed zest and energy. She happily helped Matron with lists and errands. She made a point of welcoming Meena and Shelley and introducing them both to every girl in the school with handshakes and friendly talk. She insisted that Gabriele, who really just wanted to relax into an armchair and talk about horses, help Meena to know her way around.

'You'll be given a timetable tomorrow when lessons start, Meena,' Alison explained. 'In the meantime, I'll be announcing the duty-rotas for helping in the kitchen and for answering the front door. Gabriele will show you where to put your books in the schoolroom. Gabriele?' But the Austrian girl had disappeared and was chatting in the corridor with Evangeline, swapping news from home.

'Oh honestly, Gabriele, I do wish you'd try to help out a bit.' Alison tried not to sound cross. 'It's not fair just to leave Meena to be with Renu. She's part of our group in the Upper School and it's our responsibility to help her settle in.'

Gabriele, apologising, ambled down the corridor to give Meena a warm smile. 'I'm so sorry. I think I am still not sure if I am back at school or if there is a part of me that is still at home,' she said. 'Please forgive me. Let's go and see the schoolroom.' She led the way, suddenly turning to ask, 'By the way, are you interested in horses?'

Meena had never ridden in her life and was slightly scared of them but did not like to say so. 'No, well, not specially,' she said and then hurriedly added, when she saw the disappointment in Gabriele's face, 'But of course I love them. Who couldn't? They're beautiful and graceful. And we've got some in the school field haven't we? When can we go and see them?'

This was the way to Gabriele's heart, and to Alison's too. Half an hour later, when Alison could be torn away from Head Girl duties, the three, joined by Shelley and Elizabeth, wrapped themselves against the evening chill and ran down towards the field with carrots in their hands, cheerfully given by Mrs Drummond from the kitchen.

'Gorgeous, gorgeous Mountjoy,' said Alison, greeting her favourite horse which she had now been riding regularly. 'Did you miss me? We're back and I'll be down to see you every day from now on, and riding you as often as I can.'

Meena, finding that the animals were not so scary when you knew how to approach them, reached out her hand to stroke Mountjoy's glossy coat. He certainly was beautiful. So was the smaller grey standing next to him. This one looked at her as if he understood that she was a new girl and a bit shy with animals. Gently she uncurled the hand in which she had been tightly holding her carrot. She held it out tentatively. She needn't have been afraid of his teeth: he wasn't going to bite her. Instead, she liked the brief soft wet feel of his mouth and the good crunching sound as he enjoyed every mouthful of carrot.

She turned with shining eyes to the other girls.

'What's his name? Isn't he super? Do they live here all the time and can we come to see them whenever we like?'

'Of course,' said Alison. 'He's called King, by the way. And he likes you, doesn't he? Go on, give him another gentle stroke – on the side of his head, not on his nose, as it makes it sore if you do that. He's friendly. The field belongs to the school. Naturally, other people come along and take them out; it's a very popular riding school. We can only get out here in between lessons and all the other things we have to do at school! But isn't it wonderful just having them here, knowing they're part of our lives?'

Gabriele had already fed her carrot to Felix, the horse that she had been riding regularly before half-term. She talked to him softly in her own language and in English. 'He under-stands me whatever language I use,' she said with a laugh when the other girls teased her. 'We're going to have some good rides together over the next few weeks, aren't we boy?'

They all stood talking and enjoying the company of the horses before reluctantly turning back towards the house, where soon the bell would ring for supper. Any tension between them had gone and they were fast becoming friends. Four Winds looked welcoming with its glowing windows and the promise of a good meal. Gabriele found herself slowly slipping back into the rhythm of its life again. Meena felt warm and excited by the prospect of a new school and a new challenge, Elizabeth was glad to have her friend with her, and Alison found that her cares and worries as Head Girl had given way to a sense of comradeship and relaxation. It was good to be back.

Supper was a talkative meal. Shelley caught Elizabeth's eye as they started with Grace. This was something that had never happened at their old school. She stared at the girls who were on kitchen-duty and hurried about in white aprons. But the food was good and she found she enjoyed it.

'Over the next few days you'll find out why it's so good,' said Elizabeth. 'Mrs Drummond's been running the hotel catering for years and really knows about it. She's always keen to try something new and she'll start asking you what you know about cookery. You'll find yourself joining in without even realising it. Do you do much cooking at home?'

'Well, no, not really. I've never even thought about it. And you know we never bothered with cookery at Mentlesham Heights because the lessons were always just noisy and silly. No one took it seriously. You're not really made to cook whole meals here?'

'No, it's not like that. We help out in the kitchen – it's got all the latest equipment, so there's no drudgery – and we also get cookery lessons, in small groups. Then we eat what we've made. Either it's a snack at teatime or it's part of a main meal. It's a rule that no one's allowed to be rude about it, but they do actually manage to make their views known! I've never had a major disaster yet because Mrs Drummond's really in charge. It's all so completely different from Mentlesham that you just can't compare it.'

'You can say that again.' Shelley stared round at the panelled walls and the thick curtains. 'It just doesn't feel like a school at all!'

'Well, that's because it isn't one! This was the village's big hotel until we came along! Now come on, there's lots more to show you.'

Shelley enjoyed her first evening, and when Aunt Win announced that the telephone was available to anyone who wanted to contact home, she was first in the queue to tell her grandmother and later her mother all about it. 'I can't really describe it all,' she said. 'It's just, well, it's just so unlike anywhere I've been before. But Elizabeth Hurry's here too and she's been showing me round. Yeah, yeah, I'm really all right. Having a lark, so far!'

Lessons the next day brought her down to earth with a bump. She realised how far behind she was in many subjects, and was almost in despair when she discovered how much she was supposed to cover and the standard of work expected. But then the English lesson began and Aunt Win started to read aloud some war poetry from 1914, explaining

139

about the young soldier-poets going into battle. She gave them just enough of the history to set the scene – the young men from the towns and villages, including those whose names were now on the village War Memorial, the hopes and dreams they carried and the courage and bravery that they were so anxious to show. Then came the carnage of battle – the sickening assaults of machine-gun fire, the bodies stuck fast on barbed wire, the terrible wounds, the mud and the misery. The room was quiet. The younger girls were working next door and from outside came the faint sounds of bird-song as a hint of Spring came to the wintry garden. Alison, Meena, Gabriele and Elizabeth sat with Shelley round one big table. There were still no conventional desks at Four Winds and they were using the beautiful hotel furniture. Aunt Win spoke in a low voice. There was no need for her to raise it to get everyone's attention as the group was small.

'If I should die, think only this of me
That there's some corner of a foreign field that is forever
England ...'

It was a beautiful poem and everyone was quiet for a moment after they had finished reading it. Then, slowly, Aunt Win opened up a discussion about it. They went on to read some poems by Wilfred Owen and by Siegfried Sassoon. By the time the lesson ended, Shelley felt as if she had been trans-ported for a while to another world. She found she was even looking forward to doing her homework. They were each to choose a poem, copy it out and write a short account of why they had made the choice, as well as discovering something about its author. In the ordinary way this would have seemed a boring thing to do, but instead Shelley found herself think-ing that the problem was that it would be hard to choose from among the marvellous verses they had been given. She was thoughtful, as well as hungry, when they all clattered downstairs for morning coffee.

'Well, how do you feel about your first taste of Four Winds?' asked Elizabeth, sipping from her mug and leaning back against the bannisters to talk.

'It's OK.' Shelley was guarded. 'Actually, I liked that last lesson. There's a lot to do, though, isn't there? I can sort of feel the work piling up.'

'Mmm, you're right. But in a funny way, you don't get the pressure that we used to get at the old place. I mean, here it's all individual. You don't feel so, well, hassled somehow. It's quieter, for one thing. And I just don't get that sudden urge to drop it all and get away.'

Elizabeth had never spoken like this before, not even to herself. Suddenly she found that, because of Shelley, she was having to think out her own attitude to Four Winds.

'What do we do at lunchtime? Another very official meal, with Grace and all that?'

'Yes, a lot of all that! And remember about the days when it's French and German! I've thought about that for you, and we'll write down something for you to say – just one sentence about the weather or something. No,' she held up her hand as Shelley started to protest, 'you just wait and see. You think you just won't join in and you'll prove, something by talking in English, but it just doesn't work that way. I tried it and it all falls flat. The rule is that if someone speaks in English everyone has to shut up and be absolutely silent for three minutes. That's really, really boring. Everyone glares at you.' She drew Shelley slightly away from the other girls. 'It's sort of a matter of pride,' she said in a lower voice. 'Those twins are Mrs Ontwin's nieces – nice kids but, well, you know. And then there's all these foreign girls. We can't let them get the better of us. So let's show them we can do anything as well as they can!'

Shelley needn't have worried. Everyone was keen to help her in every way. Before the French lunch, Marie, Bernadette and Evangeline, after a brief talk together, came running up to offer their help.

'We want to help you speak our tongue,' said Marie, 'so we help. Mrs Ontwin says this. And we decide on something simple. So: the weather! So English. Today is sunny. That is easy. "Il fait du soleil." You can say this? It is only four words.' They helped her to repeat it, wrote it out, explained exactly what it meant and said it with her several times.

'Il fait du soleil.' Shelley muttered it again and again to herself as they went into lunch. Evangeline had been chosen to say Grace. There was a silence as everyone sat down, and then Marie said something to Aunt Win, who responded with a smile. Marie kicked Shelley under the table. Like a machine that had been switched on, Shelley turned to Aunt Win and said, 'Il fait du soleil.' She was rewarded by a warm smile and a friendly response. She found she even understood what the headmistress had said: 'Oui, c'est bon, n'est-ce pas?' 'Yes, it's good, isn't it?' And someone across the table added a remark about the birds in the garden and how lovely they had sounded during the poetry lesson. She missed most of that, except for the word for birds which she vaguely remembered from a half-hearted attempt to work at French about a year ago. But she didn't care. She had made it! She had joined in! She was speaking French at a meal!

For some reason, even though she remained silent for the rest of the meal except to say 'Oui' when someone offered her some water, she felt exultant. 'I can do this!' she found herself thinking. 'I'm not going to be beaten by anybody!'

She wasn't, either. That afternoon it was discovered that she excelled at netball. In the kitchen that evening she found that she had a natural skill at cookery and a real interest in it. The superbly-equipped kitchen was also a warm and welcoming place, with a sense of order and purpose. The girls were taught about the cost of different ingredients and how to plan and budget meals, as well as how to cook them. The idea was that anyone who went to school at Four Winds would be independent, able to cook and look after herself, and run a house and entertain friends as part of her life skills. Learning cookery was done in an organised way and it was treated as seriously as any other subject, and the girls themselves were the severest critics of anything that tasted wrong! Mrs Drummond praised Shelley's skill at making a creamy sauce, and was delighted to have a pupil who enjoyed not only the fun and friendship of the kitchen sessions – everyone liked that – but also the real craft of cooking and planning meals.

Only after homework was over and everyone dispersed to do whatever they wanted in the free time before bed, did Shelley discover a problem. She had missed her favourite television programme and found that she was going to end up missing it every day, as it clashed with the evening activities.

'Hey, that's not fair!' she said, when the subject came up for general discussion. 'I really need to see it. I've been following it all the time from the beginning. How will I find out what's going on?'

'Sorry,' said Alison. 'Actually, none of us likes the rule very much but there it is. No television on weekdays until everything else is finished, and not then if it's something Mrs Ontwin doesn't think is suitable. We tried videoing everyone's favourite programme and saving it all up for the weekend, but that doesn't work either because we never have time to watch it all!'

'And no one could agree on what to watch first and we'd waste time arguing,' added Gabriele, 'so in the end we find that somehow we do not watch it very much at all. The only thing you can say is that, truly, after a few days you won't miss it. This evening we are free, but mostly there is not a moment. There is music practice and these First Aid classes, and once a week we have to go to the science laboratory – by car, in two groups – and then sometimes we have a meeting or some other thing to plan. It's ridiculous but there it is!'

Shelley opened her mouth to say more but thought better of it. She couldn't believe they really couldn't watch TV. Crossly, she wandered to the window to think up a plan. Elizabeth was a day-girl for part of the time and went home at weekends. Couldn't she go with her sometimes to watch TV? Would Mrs Hurry video every episode of 'Strangers', the soap opera she specially loved, so that they could watch it all on Saturday nights? That might not be too bad.

Elizabeth was busy in her own room, and before setting out to put the plan to her, Shelley stood at the window, looking out and thinking about it. Gradually, as her eyes got used to the dark, she found she could pick out the shapes of horses in the field beyond.

'Look at the horses out there,' she said. 'We really are in the country, aren't we?'

'Tell you what,' said Alison eagerly, 'early tomorrow morning come with us when we go to feed them. We go every day, just to say hello and to give them a carrot or something. Mountjoy's perfect. We all have riding lessons. Yours is

143

on Wednesday. Come and make friends with all the horses tomorrow so they'll all know you really well. Mountjoy is a perfect horse.'

'So's King,' said Meena.

'And Felix,' said Gabriele, not to be outdone. 'He's the one you should ask to ride, Shelley. I ride him sometimes but he is so gentle that he likes to meet new people and he makes friends quickly.'

In spite of herself, Shelley felt a glow. Thoughts of TV went from her mind for a moment. It was lovely to be in a place that was like a big country hotel, with horses at the bottom of the garden.

'Does the school own them?'

'No, I wish we did!' said Alison. 'They're owned by a local riding school, and it's all part of the deal that they use our field. It means we all get riding lessons. Dress quickly when you hear the rising-bell tomorrow. We'll meet at the top of the stairs and get ten minutes with the horses before breakfast.'

Chapter 16

As the weather got warmer, Aunt Win started making summer plans. A team of men came to look at the swimming pool, drain it and clean it and make it ready for use. This attracted a lot of interest, with the girls watching from windows because the pool area was out of bounds.

Sport became more important in the life of the school, and with Shelley such a strong member of the team, Aunt Win started asking her opinion about the chances of Four Winds competing against other schools. Miss Crisp, who taught maths, had been taking the girls for games and was part of the discussion too.

'I think it would be quite possible to arrange a couple of friendly matches with St John's, the big girl's school where I taught a couple of years ago,' she ventured. 'They aren't very far away and we could offer to host a match here. We'd need to practise a bit. What do you think?'

Shelley was aware that Four Winds had not been able to organise itself into proper teams as there just hadn't been enough pupils. She loved netball and the other girls seemed keen enough. But were they able to win a match?

'Well', she said cautiously, 'Let's give it a couple of weeks good work first. Would it be this school's first-ever match of any kind against another school?'

'It certainly would,' smiled Aunt Win. 'We're simply not able even to think about getting involved with serious competitions in sport yet. But we perhaps ought to make a bit of a start. All right, shall we discuss this again in two weeks' time, Miss Crisp? We'll make our decision then.'

In the cleaning-up of the swimming-pool area, the workmen opened up the sunlounge that had been locked all winter. It was now given a thorough cleaning and airing. Halfway through the morning, one of the men brought to Aunt Win an envelope, sealed, with 'A Poem for Four Winds' written on the outside.

'I found this tucked into the window-ledge,' he said. 'I don't know what it's all about but we thought we ought to bring it to you.'

Aunt Win opened the envelope and found a piece of paper, dated about four years earlier, on which a guest at the hotel had written a poem. At the top was written, 'As a thank-you to this lovely place for a peaceful and beautiful weekend, I'm writing a message: these verses. Four Winds has relaxed and inspired me. I came here needing a holiday and I found just what was right: peace and beauty and a friendly group of people.' Then followed a poem.

Aunt Win read the poem and did not think it very good. She knew and loved really beautiful poetry and these simple verses were hardly to be compared with Wilfred Owen or Rupert Brooke. But the straightforward words nevertheless amused and moved her. She took the paper to Mrs Drummond and asked her if she had any idea who might have written it.

'Well, I suppose it could have been any of the guests,' said Mrs Drummond, pausing in her peeling of apples for apple-pie. 'They all used to sit out there in the sun-lounge and enjoy the view. No, I can't say I ever remember a lady writing poetry. Sometimes I'd get talking to the guests and they'd chat about this and that but, no, think as I might, I just can't recall any face that might have belonged to a poet!'

So the mystery remained. Aunt Win kept the poem in her room, feeling that she didn't want to throw it away.

Later that day there was a clash between Miss Crisp and Shelley. Despite their friendship over netball, the two did not get on very well because Shelley loathed maths and did not make any pretence about it. She made a half-hearted attempt to take an interest in the first lesson but by the second had decided that this was one thing about Four Winds that she was just going to hate. Miss Crisp was a good teacher but

146

Shelley was far behind in this subject, and was joined in this by Gabriele who had a tendency to be lazy. The problem was increased by the fact that Meena was good at maths and positively enjoyed it.

'Great, Meena! You've really grasped it!' exclaimed Miss Crisp with obvious enthusiasm when Meena had shyly but correctly drawn out the solution to a problem. 'Now, let's take this through once again. Shelley, are you listening?' Shelley wasn't. She was looking dreamily out of the window and thinking about the horses. Idly, she drew a sketch of a horse's head on a piece of scrap paper. It wasn't very good and she squinted at it, trying to get a better perspective. Gabriele, sitting next to her, added a few lines – a bridle, some alteration around the horse's eye and mouth – and the thing began to look better. They weren't speaking but just doodling and enjoying a silent companionship.

'Shelley, I was speaking to you.'

'Oh, sorry.' She sat up and tried to look interested. Miss Crisp went on with the lesson but Shelley, her pleasant dreaming-time shattered, felt cross. Sulkily, she felt that maths just wasn't her subject. When Miss Crisp was not looking, she stealthily removed a magazine from underneath her maths book and began reading it.

Miss Crisp was busy with Meena for some while and then turned to Elizabeth and to Alison, whose work was untidy but showed signs that she had grasped what was going on. Gabriele, bored, made a sign to Shelley to move closer and share her magazine. It was not the sort of magazine that normally interested Gabriele, or the sort that Aunt Win allowed into the school. Gabriele knew that if the headmistress saw it she would confiscate it at once, but this gave reading it a spice that was lacking in the quiet schoolroom where everyone else was struggling with maths. Soon, she and Shelley were both deep in an article about fashions.

Gradually, both became aware of a very deep and uncomfortable silence. Gabriele looked up. Miss Crisp was looking down at her and holding out her hand. Shelley also started up, embarrassed.

'I'll take the magazine, I think,' said Miss Crisp in a rather cool voice. 'And you will get on with your lesson – if you've been paying enough attention to make head or tail of it, which I rather doubt.'

Of course, neither girl was able to make any sense of it at all. The more Miss Crisp asked questions and drew diagrams to explain what she meant, the more it became clear that neither Shelley nor Gabriele had been paying attention for some time.

'I think,' said Miss Crisp, 'that at the end of this lesson it might be as well for you both to go to Mrs Ontwin and explain to her why you aren't bothering with maths. Just to make things more straightforward, I'll give her this magazine and let her know this is what you would rather be doing.' Her voice sounded hurt as well as angry. Shelley felt very uncomfortable. She had liked Miss Crisp and they had got on well over the netball.

'Oh no, please, I …' she wanted to say she was sorry but it was all obviously too late. The buzzer went and Miss Crisp took the magazine and her own stack of books and left the room. A babble of talk broke out.

'Honestly Shelley, you're mad!' said Elizabeth. 'Surely you must have known there'd be a row about reading a magazine in the middle of a maths lesson!'

'Just tell Mrs Ontwin that you've found it all difficult. She will understand.' Meena tried to be kind and encouraging.

'I'll help you, if you like, to find out what the lesson was all about. It's honestly quite interesting once you get the hang of it.' Alison tried to sound positive too – after all, Shelley was a new girl – but it was hard to avoid the fact that they were in for a row.

Feeling distinctly uncomfortable, Shelley and Gabriele wondered what they were meant to do next. In a rush Shelley decided that she'd brazen it out, tell Mrs Ontwin that she hated this stupid school anyway and was going to leave. She felt hot and angry. She started to imagine the scene: the clever things she would say, how she would walk out of Four Winds – changing first out of this silly uniform – and just calmly announce at home that she'd had enough. She didn't think much beyond that. Going back to her old school? Facing her grandmother? She pushed those thoughts away. Instead, she thought about the dialogue with Mrs Ontwin.

148

'You're old-fashioned,' she would say to her. 'No television in the evenings and talking French at lunch. I ask you, is it normal? You're just running a weird freak school. I'm off – and I'll get a government inspector round to say that you're running a hopelessly inadequate school where the girls do nothing but cookery and haven't even got proper desks.'

She began to feel rather proud of herself. She ran through the scene again. Would she knock on Mrs Ontwin's door or just walk in, strong and determined? Perhaps she would simply write it all in a note and leave it behind when she left? But then she wouldn't be able to see everyone's faces when they heard about it.

Gabriele felt rather less certain. There had been a problem once or twice before, and she had been ticked off about some Latin homework handed in late and cookery notes not written up properly. She didn't want to take home a bad report. Her parents would not find it amusing.

'Gabriele! Shelley! Mrs Ontwin asked me to send for you. Apparently you're wanted for something downstairs.' It was Jeannie, who was on door-duty that day and had answered Aunt Win's call to take a message. She evidently didn't know that there was any trouble, as she gave them her normal smile as she hurried off to her own next lesson. Elizabeth gave Shelley a good-luck sign as she left the room to make her way downstairs.

Outside Mrs Ontwin's room the clever arguments didn't sound so smart as Shelley went over them in her mind. Everything felt very quiet. Lessons had started again upstairs. Both girls could hear the sound of Alison's piano and knew that the younger girls were having geography while Meena and Elizabeth completed some history work begun yesterday.

Gabriele looked at Shelley, raised her hand to knock on Mrs Ontwin's door and let it fall again. Then they decided to get things over with, knocked and walked in. The headmistress looked up from a letter she was writing.

'I don't think I said you could come in yet, dear,' she said coolly. 'Wait outside and knock again, and don't come in until you hear me answer.'

Outside, both girls waited, knocked again and heard Mrs

149

Ontwin say, 'Wait just a moment.' So they waited. After what seemed a long time, Mrs Ontwin called, 'All right, I've finished now. Please come in.'

They felt at a disadvantage. Mrs Ontwin looked calm, relaxed and businesslike. She had finished her letters and they were sealed and ready to post. She was sitting back in her chair with the magazine on the desk in front of her, still folded.

'Now, why were you so rude to Miss Crisp?' she asked.

'But I wasn't!' Shelley said indignantly. 'I didn't say anything rude to her. Just go and ask the others.'

'No, you didn't say anything. You simply sat there during her lesson, blatantly ignoring her, reading a magazine you had brought in deliberately. Not rude at all? How would you feel if someone sat reading some magazine while you were trying to talk to them?'

Shelley fell silent. She hadn't really thought of it like that. Mrs Ontwin had rather more to say, too. Quite calmly, she spoke about Miss Crisp, the other girls in the class, the importance of lessons, and finally the nastiness of the magazine that the two girls had been reading. By the end both girls were in tears. Shelley very badly wanted to say how hard she had found the maths lesson and to beg for another chance, but she'd never be able to say it all now. Everything had gone wrong. Then, unexpectedly, Mrs Ontwin said it for her.

'In fact, Miss Crisp tells me that the lesson had not gone well from the start, and that she'd like to start you off on some simpler material anyway,' she said. 'She wants to forget all this and make a fresh start. That would be the best way, wouldn't it?'

'Oh, yes!' breathed Shelley, feeling that a burden had been lifted. 'Yes it would.'

'And for me too,' said Gabriele. 'I'm sorry. I like Miss Crisp. I had no wish to be rude.'

'Well, how do you think we should go about it? Would it help, do you think, if you sat down now and wrote a nice note of apology?' Both girls nodded, Shelley scrambling for a handkerchief. Mrs Ontwin looked at her gravely. 'Good. You will explain, too, that the magazine has been confiscated and that you know such things must not be brought into this house or read by any of the girls. You'll write the letter in your best handwriting and show it to me before handing it to Miss Crisp.' She got out a sheet of headed notepaper with the school's address on it.

'Sit out here where I can see you, and write at the hall table. No talking. I'll leave the door open so I can see you at work.'

Gabriele had thought the letter would be easy but it was surprisingly hard to write. She felt particularly silly having to admit in writing that the magazine had been confiscated. She didn't know how to end the letter. In the end she repeated how sorry she was and added, 'I really would like to make a fresh start. I didn't mean to be rude.' Should she put 'Best wishes' or 'Yours sincerely'? And how did you spell 'sincerely'? She stared at the page, trying to make a decision. Shelley had been writing swiftly but had made several false starts. They looked up at each other but caught a glimpse of their headmistress who was working at her desk and raised her head to see them from time to time. She would hear any whisper. It felt humiliating sitting there. Anyone who came by would know they were in some sort of disgrace. They both wanted their letter finished quickly. Eventually the work was done. They took the results in to Mrs Ontwin.

She read each letter through, corrected a spelling mistake – which she made Shelley write out three times on a piece of scrap paper so she'd remember it again – and gave them back to the girls.

'Here you are,' she said. 'The buzzer will go in a minute and Miss Crisp will come downstairs. Wait outside and hand it to her. Be extremely polite. You might start by apologising. I shall be listening. Then stand and wait to see what she has to say to you. Then we can consider this whole incident closed.' She held out her hand. 'Shake on it.' They shook hands.

Two minutes later the buzzer went. Blushing furiously, Shelley handed her note to Miss Crisp, who had evidently been half-expecting it, as she took it from her gravely and put down her books while she read it through. Shelley stammered out her apologies. Gabriele passed her own letter over and gulped and made her own apology. Miss Crisp

151

treated the whole thing with seriousness, read the letters, glanced through to Aunt Win and nodded.

'That's perfectly all right, and I'm very happy to make a fresh start,' she said. 'Let's shake hands. And for your next maths lesson, I'll prepare something that we can both work through together.' She smiled. Shelley, who had been crying again, managed a watery smile in return. It was all over. Next time they met, it would be all right.

After lunch, inevitably they discussed the whole incident with Elizabeth and with Meena, who had proved unexpectedly sympathetic.

'Mrs Ontwin can be fierce, but in a funny way she's quite fair,' said Elizabeth. 'You keep wanting to stay angry with her and then you can't. Coming down to see the horses? Alison said the crocuses are out on the lawn, too.'

As they ran out across the lawn, Shelley felt that, more than before, she truly belonged in this school. She had a deep-down feeling that she wanted to do well, to soar to the very top, to give of her very best always.

Chapter 17

Two days later a telephone call from the Ministry of Defence brought shattering news to Four Winds.

'Mrs Battle, I am afraid we have grave news,' said the kindly but official voice of a senior Army officer. 'We have to inform you that the Reconnaissance Group Unit which your husband is commanding has not been in radio contact with its headquarters for forty-eight hours. We will keep you fully informed, of course. There is no reason to suspect anything tragic has occurred but ...'

Aunt Win, bravely keeping her control, broke the news to Matron and to Mrs Drummond. She also sent at once for Jeannie and Geraldine and told them of the danger facing their uncle.

Matron and all the other staff were immediately kind and supportive. Matron undertook to tell the girls the news. It would not be fair for Aunt Win to have to take prayers that morning. She spoke first to Alison and then to all the other girls.

'I know I don't need to have to tell you how serious this could be. Of course we will all do our best to make things easy for Mrs Ontwin. She will not be taking lessons this morning, at least until the coffee break. Another telephone call from the Ministry of Defence is expected with the latest developments, if there are any, in the next hour. Let's make this the very special subject of our prayers today.'

The school did pray, quietly and sincerely, for Major Ontwin and for all the young soldiers under his command. Alison's thoughts had flown at once to that young officer,

Lieutenant Darrington, Andrew Darrington with his good manners and his friendly smile, his cheerful self-assurance and the way in which he seemed so eager to be off on the expedition, so certain that it would be successful. She found that a picture of his face came quickly into her mind and stayed there, coming between her and the book she was meant to be reading in French, and the chart of kings and queens in history.

At coffee-time everyone gathered to hear the news on the radio. Aunt Win had been listening in her office and now Matron brought her own radio into the girls' sitting-room.

'There has been no further news of the British Army group, missing for two days in a remote African district of Lumpoepo during the British goodwill reconnaissance mission,' announced the newsreader. 'A Ministry of Defence spokesman said that the situation was serious. Our Military Correspondent reports ...'

All that day there was a sense of concern and anxiety. Then on the evening news came a sudden and dramatic development.

'There are reports that the British army team missing in Lumpoepo is in contact with a local rebel group known to be involved with terrorism. It is not clear whether they have been captured by the terrorists or have simply established links with them after getting lost in the remote desert area. We will bring you further news as it develops.'

It was impossible, now, not to watch television! Aunt Win herself had been watching the bulletins all day and came up to the girls' room to share it with them for the late news. She had received another telephone call from the Defence Ministry.

'We're still not quite clear what is going on, Mrs Battle. The situation is very confused. This rebel group appears to be trying to put out some sort of statement by radio but their communications are very poor. We just don't know what's going on. We fear the men may have been taken as hostages but we can't confirm anything. We'll be sending an officer down to see you, if possible, to give you all the background information we can. I'm so sorry we just haven't been able to find out more.'

The girls admired their headmistress. While obviously terribly worried, she remained calm. 'Harry would not want me to panic,' she had been saying to herself. She knew that everyone at Four Winds was praying. Members of her family had telephoned to let her know that she was surrounded by their love and care. She had had difficulty in persuading Grandma that there was no need for her to come over.

'No, wait,' she had said. 'If things get worse I might need you. Just now I'd rather cope on my own. I've got Matron here and the girls are being marvellous. Let's take things one step at a time. Just keep praying.'

The TV news suddenly blared out as everyone gathered around the set.

'A sudden twist to developments in the remote African area of Lumpoepo. It appears that a British Army unit is in the hands of a bandit terrorist group known as the Lumpoepo Spiders, but it is not clear whether they are hostages or are with the group of their own free will. A tape-recorded message has just been received in the Lumpoepo capital, Impoepo. We go now, live, to Africa.'

The screen was blurred and the line poor and crackling. A reporter was in Impoepo where local conditions were evidently very primitive.

'This is the only town of any size in this huge and remote territory,' he said. 'News travels slowly but the tape recorded message, now relayed over the local radio, appears to indicate some confusion over just what has happened to the British Army team.' Then there was a pause and a different voice – blurred, crackling but definitely that of a British solder – came across. 'We are with the Lumpoepo Spiders. We are alive and well. Tell the Four Winds!' That was all.

At Four Winds there was an explosion of excitement.

'That's us!'

'What did he mean?'

'Four Winds! He said Four Winds!'

Aunt Win had, uncharacteristically, burst into sudden and silent tears. She turned quickly away so the girls wouldn't see. Jeannie and Geraldine, who had been sitting next to her, flung their arms around her.

In all the uproar the twins had difficulty making their

155

voices heard. Finally Jeannie had had to shout. 'It's a message!' she said 'Listen to me! Oh, do listen, Aunt Win! It's a message. I promise you. That was Lieutenant Darrington's voice and it was a coded message saying they need help! Honestly! We've got to telephone the Army people immediately!'

It took some time before Aunt Win really understood what she was saying. Geraldine and Jeannie both talked at once but were finally able to make themselves clear and told the story, desperate to make her understand.

'It was when all the soldiers came here – you remember – for the training. We were on tea-duty and we were talking to him. And he said – well it was sort of a joke but it isn't a joke now, it simply can't be – he said that if anything ever happened he would somehow send a message and it would be something like "Tell the Four Winds". And we promised to remember!'

Again there was an uproar as everyone talked at once. Matron called for calm. Quickly she extracted both twins from the group and got them and Aunt Win out of the room and into the corridor where she made the girls tell the whole story again.

'Honestly, I know it sounds crazy but it really did happen like that! Please, please telephone the Ministry of Defence! I just know that this is serious.' Geraldine clenched and unclenched her hands with excitement and with desperation to make Aunt Win understand.

Aunt Win, having heard the full story, headed straight for the telephone. With a twin on either side – they couldn't bear to be separated from her – she got through to the special telephone number in London.

'Yes, yes, this could make sense,' came the calm voice at the other end when Aunt Win had told her extraordinary story. 'We had assumed it was some kind of a code. It seems likely that this young officer was supposed to be making a propaganda broadcast – you know, the terrorists trying to convince the world that the British Army had joined them voluntarily for a few days and supported their cause. Any obvious attempt to tell the world what was really going on would have been hopeless. He probably had a gun at his head. But this message got through as it just sounded harmless. He's a brave young man and a clever one!'

Then things happened quickly. Back at the headquarters base of the Army expedition, an anti-terrorist unit was swiftly armed and sent on its way. Kept in touch by radio, the Ministry of Defence was able to learn something of its progress. Late into the night, Aunt Win sat waiting for news. She had insisted that the school go to bed as normal. Matron allowed Alison and the twins to sit up for a while but then sent them off, too. They knew that the only right thing to do in a crisis such as this – where they could do nothing to help, back here in the English countryside – was to be sensible. Jeannie and Geraldine lay in bed, tense and worried. They had said their prayers many times over. Their thoughts flew to Africa. They couldn't imagine what it must be like to be held hostage in a distant desert region.

All next day the tension remained. Aunt Win spoke on the telephone to the families of the other members of Uncle Harry's team, including young Lieutenant Darrington's mother. 'Yes,' she said to her, 'it was a simple message to my two nieces, who are pupils at my school here. They were chatting to him when he arrived for the training exercise. I think it was just a joke between them. Yes, yes, very sensible and nice children. Yes, I'll pass on your message to them. Yes, yes of course. Let's all be brave. God bless you.'

Lessons continued as normal, although afterward no one remembered much about what they had studied. Newspapers and radio stations kept telephoning and Mrs Hurry took over in Aunt Win's office, dealing with them all. She and Aunt Win had written out a statement: 'Mrs Battle is grateful for everyone's concern. She is in touch with some of the other wives and family members of the soldiers on the expedition. They are all determined to be brave and they are following every moment of the rescue mission.'

Late in the afternoon, Matron insisted that the usual ballet practice session be held, even though everyone just wanted to sit around and talk. She was right; it was better to be active. Somehow, the music and the exercise helped. Later, Jeannie was always to associate some of the music that had been played with the mood of that particular afternoon.

Then, just before supper, the news broke.

'They're free! The whole team has been rescued! Our British rescue mission found the terrorist headquarters, surrounded it, and finally broke in. They've found the men, and I've just heard they've all been accounted for!'

Aunt Win was exultant. She whirled around the room, taking first Geraldine's hands and then Jeannie's in a crazy and joyful dance.

Telephones started ringing. A TV team arrived at the house.

'Better tidy up and go and face them.' Matron fussed around Aunt Win, helping her to do her hair. Matron McMurdoch, normally so calm, efficient and brisk, had herself burst into tears on hearing the news that all was well. Now she was making up for it by being more than usually businesslike. She shooed everyone into the schoolroom to be out of the way when the TV company arrived. Then she relented and let them be filmed giving a tremendous cheer and applause, all standing on the stairs. They couldn't wait to see themselves on television that evening.

Most exciting of all, the twins were interviewed for television. 'Four Winds – an unusual name for a school,' said the interviewer, a smiling man with tousled brown curly hair and a casual, easy way of talking in front of the TV cameras. 'Now, tell me what actually happened when you met Lieutenant Darrington and he gave you this special code-word?'

'Well, we just got talking when he came here, you see,' said Geraldine shyly. 'And then – really just as a sort of joke – he said that if they ever got into any difficulties in Africa he'd send a message. He'd say something like "Tell the Four Winds" and we'd know that we were to get help immediately.'

'We didn't think it was for real, and he didn't either,' said Jeannie. 'It was just all for fun at the time. We'd been making scones in the cookery lesson, you see, and were just setting out the cups and plates for tea, and he was talking to our Uncle Harry in the hall.' Talking in front of a TV camera felt strange and rather silly, because the interviewer kept nodding and smiling and had a microphone pinned on his tie and a tiny earphone carefully fitted behind his ear and held in place with sticking-plaster, but it was nevertheless fun to see themselves on the screen later on.

Newspaper reporters also arrived and took photograph after photograph. The next day's newspapers carried big headlines saying 'The school that became an emergency code-word!' and 'Twin schoolgirls link with African rescue!' It was all very exciting. The newspapers particularly liked the fact that the girls were twins and described Jeannie as a 'pigtailed brunette' and Geraldine as a 'curly-topped redhead'. Both were described as 'lively youngsters whose quick-thinking saved the day' and 'smiling schoolgirls who helped ensure a rescue team arrived in time'.

There were excited telephone calls from Japan as the news stories went across the world and all the Brown family shared in the thrill of finding themselves suddenly famous.

There were pictures of the twins, grinning and looking pleased with themselves, standing by the school notice-board which had 'Four Winds' clearly written above it in Alison's best lettering. Just faintly behind them, you could also see notices about kitchen rotas and riding-lessons, and one from Matron about putting shoes away tidily.

Being in the news can make you feel terribly important for a while, and both girls found the next couple of days very exciting. Ordinary lessons seemed quite unimportant. Then, as suddenly as it had happened, the story died down. From being celebrities, the twins were ordinary schoolgirls again.

'Salvete, Ut vales?' Father Higgins said at the beginning of his Latin lesson as usual, and the girls answered him with the Latin phrases they now knew 'Optime, valeo!' or 'Bene!'' Sitting at the table, her Latin book in front of her, Jeannie felt that everything seemed ordinary and dull. She found herself idly swinging her leg to kick it against the table-leg and drawing squiggles on her notebook. Eventually Father Higgins, who never needed to tell anybody off because his lessons were always interesting, had to tell her quite sharply to stop and get on with her work. At lunch-time, too, the mood had changed. The African adventure was over now and the girls were busy talking about other things. It was really quite a lesson in how quickly you can stop being a celebrity. Later, talking about it, both twins admitted to each other that although it had been fun being in the news, its was somehow rather reassuring to be back to normal again.

But of course the whole adventure wasn't really over yet, as the soldiers had yet to arrive back from Africa. They had all announced that, despite their ordeal, they were determined to stay on and finish the project they had been sent out to achieve. They were to be there for a further four weeks. After rest and some medical treatment, they would be back at their tasks of mapping out the territory and working out plans for roads and bridges. While the newspaper headlines faded, their real work resumed, and with courage and dedication they got on with the job in hand.

Back at Four Winds, the older girls had of course discussed the whole story endlessly.

'Go on, admit it Alison, you just fell totally for this Andrew Darrington – a tall, goodlooking soldier, and now he's a hero!' Meena, Gabriele and Shelley teased Alison as they sat talking late one night over mugs of cocoa.

'Well, I, I suppose I did. I certainly remember the twins telling him I was Head Girl. And wishing they hadn't! But he had such a really nice smile. I must say, he is good-looking. I'd certainly like to see him again.'

They got talking about love, romance, boyfriends and marriage.

'I don't really know what I think any more,' said Shelley, whose ideas had been changing during the time she'd been at Four Winds. 'I mean, you think older people don't know anything about love. And my own parents, well, it's been horrible. They're divorced. It's all a mess. But then you see someone like Mrs Ontwin, bursting into tears because her husband's safe, and you suddenly realise they've been in love for years and years and years, and will go on being for always.'

'I just think the important thing is a person's character,' said Elizabeth feelingly. 'It's not just a bloke showing off and bragging and trying to be smart. Anyone can do that. It's knowing he's really decent, deep down. As for marriage, you'd have to be really, really sure before you made those promises.'

'In our tradition,' said Meena, 'the parents arrange the

marriages, and I think this has a lot to be said for it. Oh, I know you'll protest' – all the other girls had started to interrupt her – 'but quite honestly it makes sense. After all, your parents love you more than anyone else does. They will want a good husband who will always care for you.'

'And will you let your parents pick a husband for you, then?' asked Elizabeth and Gabriele together.

'Oh, I don't know, it's all too early yet! And I think I should choose! But when I look at my parents, I have to say that theirs is a good marriage. It was an arranged marriage. It was all planned by their parents – my grandparents – who arranged for them to meet and asked if they liked each other, and saw that they got to know each other and so on. And then when they married, it all seemed to work well. They've made a beautiful and happy home for us, much happier than some English families. Sorry, I don't want to be rude, but it's a fact.'

'Goodness, I don't even want to think about marriage yet!' said Alison suddenly, terrified. 'This just started as a conversation about boyfriends! Yes, I admit it I did find Andrew Darrington amazing. He has good manners and he's brave and everything. But I'm going to be sixteen in a couple of weeks and he seems much older!'

'Not really,' said Elizabeth. 'He's nineteen, according to the newspapers. One called him the "courageous nineteen year-old soldier". That makes him still a teenager.'

'Well, I did like him,' Alison admitted. 'And I would like to see him again.'

Chapter 18

Meanwhile, life at Four Winds had returned to normal. Aunt Win, brisk and cheerful, insisted on high standards for lessons and so it was easy to pick everything up again after the excitement. There was a discussion about a netball match and a formal invitation went to St John's. Shelley would captain the team, with Elizabeth, Geraldine, Marie, Bernadette, Joan and Renu as players. Amanda's foot was healing well but it was still best for her not to take the risk of further injury. Jeannie was too wrapped up in ballet to take more than a routine interest in sport. Evangeline shared her view and said she had never been able to understand the British enthusiasm for tossing a ball around the court in damp cold weather, and ballet was more gentle and graceful, though just as much hard work!

Plans went ahead, too, for the end-of-term concert. It would be performed twice – once, in a shortened version, for patients at the big local hospital, and then again at Four Winds in a gala performance to which family and friends were all invited. Parents would come to enjoy the concert and then take their girls home to start the Easter holidays. Everyone knew that Aunt Win would be making an announcement, too, about the future of Four Winds.

'But I know she's got things planned for the summer term,' said Elizabeth. 'It's not secret. She was talking to Matron at supper last night about the summer uniforms. She's going to show us the designs tonight. And there's even talk of some more pupils.'

'Yes, and I know some of them!' said young Renu unexpectedly. This conversation was taking place in the girls' sitting room one evening. Homework was over, Jeannie and Geraldine were practising ballet with Marie, Bernadette and Evangeline. Gabriele was making some sketches of horses at a table and Alison was working on a design for the concert programme. 'It's our cousins. My father has been so pleased with the way things have turned out for Meena and for me that he's been telling all the family. Our cousins – three of them, they live in Medchester – will be coming here as daygirls! I'm really pleased.'

'What are their names?' asked Alison, looking up from her concert programme. 'Will they be in the Upper School or the Lower School?'

'Well, one of them's got the same name as me, Renuka, but she always uses the full name, I think, so there won't be any confusion. She's about the same age as Meena, so she'll certainly be in the Upper School. Perhaps we'll just have to say there's a big Renuka and a little Renuka. You'll have to watch out for her, she's terribly brainy. She ...'

'What, even brainier than Meena?' asked Gabriele, looking up unexpectedly from her drawing.

'Oh, hush up, you!' Meena leapt to her own defence with a grin. 'Just because all you care for is horses.' The two girls had become close friends, making a threesome with Alison, and enjoyed teasing one another. The friendship was good for them all. The love of horses was something that Shelley also shared. More than once, all the older girls had run out across the garden lawns in the evening to talk to the horses before bedtime. It wasn't strictly forbidden – the house was not locked until everyone was in bed and there was no rule about not going into the grounds – but they all felt that perhaps Matron might take a dim view of pupils wandering out to the field when it was dark, even though it wasn't very late. So they kept quiet about it, and the moments snatched with the horses, out in the spring night, with the country sounds all around them, were long to remain a magic part of the memories of that first term at Four Winds.

'There'll be some other pupils too, I think,' said Alison, carrying on from where Renu had left off. 'After all that TV publicity, when we were shown in the News cheering on the stairs, Mrs Ontwin got several telephone calls from local families. They hadn't known there was a school here. They want to find out about us and I think some of them have since come to discuss sending their girls here. I saw one or two families downstairs the other day. I beamed at them and they beamed back, and one lady said how smart we all looked in our neat uniforms!'

This got them talking about other aspects of school. Four Winds didn't have a formal crest or badge. There wasn't even an official sports uniform, although that was now being changed as short red divided skirts and cream shirts had been ordered from a local shop. There was also the question of rules – school rules. Although people knew there were certain things they must and must not do, they had never been written down.

'We'll have a meeting about all this,' declared Alison, 'after Mrs Ontwin's made her announcements about uniform tomorrow. Up here in the sitting-room. Everyone to attend.'

The meeting took place the next evening in the sitting room, with everyone in chairs or on the big sofa. First, Aunt Win talked about uniforms. The plan for the summer was to continue the pinafore-dress style but in light cotton, a pale blue denim-colour of a simple design, to be worn with a white cotton open-necked shirt underneath, of long or short sleeves according to the weather. With this would go jerseys or cardigans of grey with a red strip round the cuffs.

'We'll get some made by a local firm,' said Aunt Win, 'although people can also make their own if they like, to an agreed design. Of course, you'll all need more than one dress, and these are easy to wash and will dry quickly. There are blazers too, striped blue and white. I know you will like them. I don't know about hats. They're just not really worn by most schools now. You can have a think about that, if you like. Any ideas you've got can come to me or to other members of staff and we'll bring it all back to a later meeting.'

She also informed them – although this was technical matter and would not much affect them – that a proper Board of Governors had been established for the school, and formal registration arranged according to the law. 'I'm already in touch with all your parents about this, and a good

164

plan has been put forward in which the parents will play a major role,' she said. 'There has been, I must say, such tremendous enthusiasm and support. It's all tremendously encouraging.'

On the subject of school rules she was happy for the girls to have their own discussion. 'But remember that I, and perhaps also eventually the school governors, will have the last word,' she said. 'I'd like to have your thoughts. Incorporate into them the rules we already have and the ideas on which we've so far based the school. Write it all down as you think of each item. I'll look forward to reading it.'

Alison agreed to do this, and then looked at the list of matters they needed to discuss.

'We were also wondering about a school badge,' she said tentatively. 'Can we work on that, too?'

'Of course,' said Aunt Win generously. 'All ideas welcome, but don't invent anything too elaborate. Remember someone will have to design and sew it! And again, look around you. There are already all sorts of symbols and signs associated with Four Winds. Don't start from scratch. Why not start from things we've already done or said or thought about?'

'What else should a school have?' someone asked from the sofa.

'A school song?' hazarded Renu. 'My last school had one, although nobody sang it. They just treated it as a joke.'

'Nothing here is going to be a joke in that way,' said Alison firmly. 'I don't think we can just write one, though.'

'Wait a moment,' said the headmistress, 'I've had a sudden thought! Keep on talking girls, work on the rules, or something. I'll be back! I've got something useful downstairs.' And with that she flew out of the room, leaving them all mystified.

The rules seemed a big task to tackle so they put it aside and looked at the idea of a badge first.

'Now, what's the symbol of this school?' asked Alison, applying Aunt Win's suggestion about thinking of things already connected with Four Winds. 'What have we got already that we ought to depict?'

'Red ribbons?' hazarded Amanda. 'In two stripes, like the ones we have on our dresses?'

165

'A fireplace, with people talking?' That was Meena's suggestion. She would always carry in her mind a picture of the school as she had first seen it, that terrifying stormy night. What a haven it had been – the warm hall and the bright fireplace with girls clustered around it.

'Girls in pinafores?' Everyone giggled at that.

'A signpost pointing to the Four Winds?'

The suggestions came thick and fast but none of them made any particular sense. None of them conveyed the real spirit of Four Winds which made the school what it was.

'I know,' said Amy suddenly, 'handshakes!' She was still the smallest girl in the school and rather shy about speaking up, so she blushed when everyone turned to stare at her.

'Whatever do you mean?' Gabriele started to ask, but both Shelley and Jeannie said at once, 'Yes, that's right, handshakes!'

'Well,' said Amy, her voice a bit wobbly with shyness, 'Everyone in this school shakes hands a lot. Haven't you noticed? Whenever we meet anyone new, of course, and when we make up after a quarrel, and even when we've been ticked off for something and want to make a fresh start. Mrs Ontwin makes us do it, and now so does Matron.'

'And when we do agree the school rules, I bet the first thing we do is to shake hands on it,' said Amanda. 'It's true, handshakes are the theme at this school.'

'And we're international,' Geraldine pointed out, 'so it's handshakes across international borders.

"Yes, and we in other nations sometimes shake hands even more than you English do,' said Bernadette. 'I was taught to shake hands and even to curtsey to grown-ups.'

'And we'll make it two hands coming together to form a cross,' said Alison on a sudden inspiration. She drew a rough sketch to show what she meant, with two hands joining each other with an upright post in the background. 'A bit like a signpost, with the four points of the cross showing the four points of the compass – North, South, East and West.'

'The Four Winds!' said Amanda. 'Yes, it's absolutely right!'

'And the cross is the Christian symbol too, without looking too religious,' said Gabriele thoughtfully. 'After all, as Mrs Ontwin so often says ...'

166

'We are not pagans!' shouted everyone. They had all heard their headmistress use the phrase so often!

'Well, my goodness, girls, it just couldn't be more appropriate.' The voice behind them made them turn round. They had failed to notice Aunt Win coming into the room. Jeannie and Geraldine giggled and blushed. Had she heard them all shouting out one of her favourite phrases?

If she had, she didn't seem to mind. 'I went downstairs to get a bit of paper,' she said. 'It was a poem written by someone who had been staying here. That was when Four Winds was an hotel, of course. This person, whoever it was, found it so peaceful and beautiful that he or she wrote a poem about it and tucked it into a window-seat down by the swimming pool. Just re-reading it, I think it could easily be set to music and would make a fine school song for us. The astonishing thing is that it makes exactly the same point that you have done with the badge – that the Four Winds point to the four corners of the Cross, the Christian symbol. Listen:

And she read out:

> The beauty of creation,
> Of earth and trees and sky,
> Gives praise to the Creator,
> Our God who reigns on high.
> The Four points of the compass
> A holy image make,
> Reminding us of service
> For God and neighbour's sake.
>
> At Four Winds we can honour
> The good things that we share,
> Companionship and comfort
> Where there is love and care.
> Preparing us for service
> To God and all things true,
> Reminding us to honour Him
> In everything we do.

'Now,' she went on, 'if we changed "comfort" in that third line of the second verse to "learning", so that it referred to a

167

school rather than to an hotel, doesn't it all say something rather good?'

'Yes! Yes!' everyone shouted. After much more talk, and Aunt Win reading the poem aloud again, it was agreed that Alison would find some music to which it would fit, perhaps a well-known hymn tune. In fact, she quickly found it fitted well to 'The Church's one foundation'.

The discussion on rules, when it finally took place, which was some days later, benefited from the fact that everyone had time to think about it. In the end, they took Aunt Win's advice and just wrote down the things that the school already taught.

'We need a sort of introduction, saying what the school's all about,' said Alison, pen poised over the blank sheet of paper.

'Well, let's take Mrs Ontwin's famous phrase and use that,' said Meena. 'Start with the religious principles and the rest flows. That's actually what my grandparents taught me in India, and I think it's right.'

So Alison started to write and the document slowly took shape, as everyone chipped in with ideas and inspirations, sometimes arguing with one another, sometimes getting the giggles, sometimes everyone talking at once. It all took time, and a five-minute break in the middle when Matron came in to find out what the noise was all about and insisted on everyone cooling down by imposing a five-minute complete silence for tempers to settle.

Finally, this is what the rules looked like:

1. This is Four Winds School. We are not pagans and we will honour God, pray together regularly, talk of holy things in a respectful way and practise the religion that our parents have taught us.
2. We will respect our teachers and do as they say. We will be grateful to them for the help they are giving us.
3. We will help one another, making up quickly after quarrels and treating one another always with courtesy and friendship.
4. We will take special care to be friendly to every new girl at the school, to anyone who is ill, and to people who do

168

not speak our language or who feel lonely or frightened.

5. We will wear our school uniform with pride and remember that while wearing it we are identified as Four Winds girls.

6. We will be gentle with animals and with all of nature's beauty, making sure that we make careful use of everything in God's creation.

7. We will value good music, art, culture, science and everything that makes up the fullness of life. We will do everything as well as we can, whether it is cleaning the kitchen or working at mathematics.

8. We will obey any regulations that are made from time to time about places that are out of bounds, or things we should not do.

That didn't cover everything but it said more or less what people wanted. Everyone was rather tired of the rules by the time they had agreed them, and glad when the final version was taken down to Aunt Win. She showed them to the rest of the staff and, together with some more detailed regulations that spelled out dull things like lesson-times, meal-times, bed-times, etc., they were agreed.

'What do we do with them now?' asked Jeannie, after Aunt Win had brandished the newly-typed rules at lunchtime.

'Don't let's just frame them and hang them up,' said Shelley. 'That would remind me of my old school, where we had a silly notice like that near the entrance-lobby but everyone just ignored it.'

'Well, these rules aren't going to be ignored,' said Aunt Win. 'They're important. They're a family set of rules and everyone must have a copy.' She thought for a moment. 'First, everyone can write them out, in really good handwriting. That will be done this afternoon. I'll do it too. Then, we'll all put our names in a hat and shake them all together. Whatever name you draw, that person will get your copy of the rules. Make your rules as nicely-done as possible. Put your own name at the bottom, and even a special message if you like.'

At first there were one or two groans at the idea of writing out the rules. It almost seemed like being set a punishment.

But then the idea of each girl producing a really beautiful version took hold. They didn't just spend a short time at it. The project spread over several days, with people painting, decorating and even producing illuminated lettering. In the end, the different sets of rules were a joy to behold. Meena took responsibility for shaking all the names in a hat and walked round the big circle passing it so that everyone could take one out. There were exclamations and some laughter when people discovered which names they had drawn.

'Now, we'll each hand over our rules to the person whose name we have, with a handshake!' called out Elizabeth. There was a rush of handshaking and mutual congratulations and admiration of artwork.

'As every new girl comes to the school, she will have someone allocated to her who will be her guide and friend,' said Aunt Win. 'That person will introduce her to the rules and will show her how to make her own copy. The friend will be expected to help and both girls will sign their name at the bottom.'

So the rules at Four Winds were established and, together with the school crest, were all set and in place by the time the end of term drew near.

Chapter 19

The pace of life quickened, and soon it seemed that every day brought an important event in school life.

First came the netball matches. Shelley had put tremendous energy into getting the teams trained and ready. She volunteered to hold extra training sessions – which everyone willingly attended – in between normal sports classes, and they enjoyed discussing tactics and ideas. When the new sports kit arrived, she took the lead in helping everyone to sew on name-tags, and even endured Matron's scrupulous checking of how the job was done. She was also busy in the kitchen. Now firm friends with Mrs Drummond, she enjoyed learning how to bake cakes and biscuits for what promised to be a really splendid tea. Everyone just hoped that there would be a victory to celebrate!

The match day dawned bright and clear, and when the St John's girls arrived, all the Four Winds pupils turned out to give their coach a cheer. The team captains shook hands at the beginning of the match, and the edges of the court were lined with spectators from both schools. The Four Winds girls had decked themselves out with ribbons of the school colours, red and grey-blue. Jeannie wore bright red ribbons on the ends of her plaits and a bright rosette blending both colours. She gave Geraldine a special good-luck hug before the match began.

It was hard work! The St John's girls, nimble and well-trained, proved fine opponents. The game was tense and exciting. Thanks partly to Shelley's training, the Four Winds girls were good at defending their own goal. Again and again, with speedy movements they prevented the St John's girls from scoring. A roar went up from all the onlookers as a near-goal was deftly prevented by Shelley herself in a brilliant move. She certainly was skilled! By half-time, neither side had managed to score. Then Elizabeth, leaping so eagerly that she almost tripped and fell, managed to toss the ball lightly into the net. First goal of the match to Four Winds! Renu strained her every nerve to keep her eye on the ball. Shelley and Elizabeth darted here, there and everywhere. Geraldine was at her best, cheered on by Jeannie. Everyone played well and then Renu, seizing her moment, managed to score a goal with only a few minutes to go before the end of the game. St John's failed to score. Match to Four Winds!

The St John's team were generous to the victors and gave them three hearty cheers. And now for a delicious tea! All the players and the onlookers had good appetites.

'We enjoyed the game,' the St John's captain told Shelley, 'and we don't mind losing to such good opponents, especially as you're a new school. Hope we meet again for many more matches!'

'We haven't lost a match all term!' a young St John's team member confided to the twins. 'We were certainly expecting to win. Well done you! And thanks for a lovely tea!'

The two games mistresses, St John's and Four Winds, chatted together as they were old friends.

'You seem to be enjoying teaching here, Marjorie,' the St John's teacher told Miss Crisp. 'It certainly is a charming school, in such a splendid setting. And is it true that the girls themselves helped to make the cakes and scones we're all enjoying?'

'Yes, they did. In fact Shelley, our keenest team member, is also one of our best cooks,' said Miss Crisp. 'She's a new girl – well, I suppose all our girls are new, but she only arrived a few weeks ago – and she's really entering into the spirit of things.'

Shelley heard this with real pleasure and found herself blushing red.

When the St John's girls piled into their coach to go home, everyone at Four Winds stood in the drive to cheer them again on their way.

'We'll be back!' cried their games teacher. 'Or, better still, you'll be coming to us for a return match!'

It was early evening, and Joan and Elizabeth had stayed at school late but were not staying the night so they set out to walk home together. They had done the journey so many times, first in snow and now in mild spring weather. Their red berets made a cheery splash of colour in the dusk.

'It's been fun, hasn't it?' said Joan. 'I felt so proud of you, scoring that goal.'

'Well, I felt proud of you,' said Elizabeth unexpectedly. The two sisters had not always been close but in recent weeks the life at Four Winds had drawn them together. 'And soon it's the concert and we'll both be singing together in the choir. I know Mum's invited some of her friends to come along. I just hope it doesn't make us suddenly feel daft, standing up there with everyone staring.'

'Of course it won't,' said Joan. 'It'll be like this afternoon. Everyone accepts we're a normal local school now and part of local life. Hasn't it been fun, making that happen?'

Three days before the gala concert, Uncle Harry arrived back at Four Winds to a tremendous welcome. He swept up Aunt Win in a tremendous embrace and shook every girl and teacher by the hand, with a hug for his two nieces. He was suntanned but looked thinner than they had remembered, and Aunt Win saw a tiredness round his eyes and a sense of exhaustion. But none of this spoiled the fun of the welcome that had been planned for him, with three hearty cheers as he entered the hall and many willing hands to unload his luggage and serve the celebration meal in which everyone shared.

'It was a great adventure, Win,' he said, 'but tough work. Young Darrington was courageous with that broadcast. I can't tell you what it felt like when we heard the shouting and knew that rescuers were at hand! And I can't praise too highly our own medical team, who pulled us through and also treated many of the local people who were sick. We're all safe home now. Oh, it's good to be back!'

He had been beaten up by the terrorists, as had the other members of the group, and they had been locked in a cellar with very little food and fresh air for much of the time but, once recovered, they had been determined to stay on in Lumpoepo and help the people they had originally been there to serve. The work had been completed on schedule.

Jeannie and Geraldine hadn't forgotten the almost casual remark he'd made, right back at the beginning of Four Winds, about making sure there was a special meal for a returning solider. They insisted that he was given his favourite meal (fried chicken with bacon, a fresh crunchy salad and buttered new potatoes) and a choice of delicious puddings.

All other members of the Army team were also now safely back with their families. Andrew Darrington had made a special point of saying that he wanted to return to Four Winds to thank the twins. This would be arranged before the end of term.

Then came the concert. First, the school choir and the ballet group performed in the local hospital. The ballet teacher who ran classes in the village had devised a special small dance for the Four Winds girls to perform together, and had given them extra classes so that they could learn it. The elderly patients and their friends all enjoyed it very much. They were delighted with the choir, too, especially the song 'Nymphs and shepherds' which proved so popular that it had to be sung twice. Everyone returned to Four Winds in high spirits.

Next day, parents began to arrive after lunch for the grand gala. And not only parents. First to arrive was Grandma Brown, thrilled to see how the school had developed and grown since those early days in the winter when she had driven over to help with the sewing of the uniforms. She was closely followed at the front door by another older lady, obviously also a grandmother.

'Is this the right place for the concert?' the newcomer asked. 'I've my granddaughter here, Shelley Willmot, and she told me there was a school concert today.'

'Of course, come right in!' said Grandma, delighted. 'I've got granddaughters here too, the Brown twins. Oh, I'm so delighted you're here!' And soon the two were chatting like old friends.

Next to arrive was a good-looking young man who spoke

with a foreign accent. Elizabeth was greeting people at the door and was rather taken aback when he asked for 'Countess von Trannenberg'. She wanted to say 'Oh, I don't think we've got a countess here' but checked herself in case it sounded rude. Maybe he was a madman but you had to be polite. So instead she asked him to repeat the name, and then was interrupted when Gabriele came rushing up.

'Franz! How good that you're here!' she cried, and then broke into German for their family news. 'Wie gehts? Und Wie gehts Mami und Papi?' After some moments of talk, she suddenly remembered Elizabeth and introduced her. 'Elizabeth, you've often heard me speak of my brother Franz. My parents cannot come to the concert but he is here to represent the family. Franz, this is Elizabeth who is a member of the Upper School here with me.' Elizabeth smiled and held out her hand, but instead of just shaking it, Franz raised it to his lips as Austrians do. Elizabeth felt wonderful. Soon they were all chatting away comfortably, and Franz was amused and charmed when she spoke a few words in German. He spoke English fluently and explained that he had arrived in England to work for some months at a stables in the next county.

'Perhaps Gabi has told you that our parents run a stables back in Austria,' he said, 'I hope to work in the family business some day, so I am starting here on the ground, getting all the experience I can, while also improving my English and doing some studies here in this language. So this is the famous school that Gabi has been telling us all about in her letters! Already, I seem to know all of you: the little girl who broke her toe, and the adventure of the soldiers who went to Africa! It must be fun to – how do you say it? – to start a school from scratch?' Elizabeth found herself explaining and laughing with him about how Four Winds had begun. How long ago it seemed when she first arrived as a reluctant day-girl.

The big moment for the twins came when their own familiar car came up the drive and out poured their three little brothers and their parents.

'Mummy! Daddy! You made it! Oh, it's lovely, lovely, lovely to see you again!' In moments, both twins were in their parents' arms. There was so much to say, so many things to show them! The little boys seemed so much bigger and wanted their own share of hugs and attention too. It was glorious to be a proper family again.

Alison's parents felt so proud that their daughter was Head Girl. Four Winds had done a great deal for her. In place of the shy, rather unhappy girl who had been so bullied at her old school, there was now a confident sixteen-year-old. And who was this young man, coming up to her with a handshake and a cheerful grin?

'Alison – oh, excuse me, I'm Andrew Darrington. I met Alison when I came here on an Army training exercise.' He greeted Alison's parents with courtesy and enthusiasm. They liked him immediately.

'So, you're the young man fresh from grim adventures in Africa! How good to meet you! Of course, we followed every moment on the television. Congratulations on your safe return and on a brave expedition.'

Like Uncle Harry, he was sunburned and looked thinner, but his handshake was firm and his smile as friendly as before. Alison found herself smiling back.

'I'm here to thank the twins,' he said. 'We owe our lives to them, you know. Could you let me know where I'd find them? Oh, and I'm here with my mother and sister. Susie – she's my youngest sister – may be coming to school here. I think she's excited about going to such a famous school. I must talk to the Brown twins first, but then do come and meet my family.'

Alison quickly found the twins and their parents. After warm greetings he said 'Wait!' and ran off, to return with two beautiful bouquets, one for Jeannie and one for Geraldine. 'These come from all of us in the team,' he said. 'We can't ever say thank you enough. I gather the newspapers got rather excited about the story. Well, you deserve your fame.'

They all talked excitedly, pounding him with questions about the whole adventure. He described the capture and imprisonment of the soldiers.

'It was an ambush, really. We should have been cleverer. We were lured into a trap. One of their men was working with us as a local liaison but turned out to be a spy. The

176

Lumpoepo Spiders, they called themselves: a rather grim bunch, it has to be said.' Sudden memories of the imprisonment, the beatings, the heat and the hunger swept over him and he wiped his hand briefly across his face. 'Well, it was fairly nasty. The worst came when they tried to make us do a propaganda broadcast. I was desperate to know what to do. Just refuse? Or try to get some sort of coded message across? Then I had this sudden thought about mentioning Four Winds. The terrorists obviously wanted to pretend to the world that we were with them of our own accord. We hoped that the Army authorities and the Government back here in Britain wouldn't believe that, but what could we do? Then I remembered that almost casual remark I'd made to you – just a joke really – and I used it in the broadcast. "Tell the Four Winds", I remember saying when they pushed the microphone in front of me, and hoping against hope that you might remember and know that we needed help.'

Jeannie and Geraldine broke in, telling their side of the story.

'It seemed crazy at first, almost unbelievable!' said Geraldine, thinking back to that moment when they had all been watching the television and Andrew Darrington's voice had come crackling over on the broadcast. 'We all just shouted because he'd mentioned Four Winds. Then Jeannie and I tried to start explaining.'

'And everyone talked at once and it was hard to get Aunt Win to listen,' put in Jeannie.

'And then finally we got the message across that this was really important, and the next thing we knew, she was on the telephone and, well, action started pretty quickly!'

Mrs Darrington greeted the twins almost as an old friend, and got on well with the Brown parents. Andrew called Alison over, who was also introduced. There were further handshakes all round. Susan, looking up at the Head Girl, felt in awe of her, but she got on well with the twins and was soon talking eagerly to them. She was thrilled at the thought of attending Four Winds. 'I'm going to spend the holidays pleading with my parents to let me come here! Andrew's told me all about it. He made the whole place sound the most fantastic sort of school.'

With so much talking going on, it was almost hard to start getting ready for the concert. But Matron and Aunt Win were busy organising the girls into their places and programmes were distributed to the audience. Gradually people began to take their seats, and an air of expectancy spread as Alison's rousing piano music launched the afternoon's entertainment.

The concert was a big success. Jeannie poured herself into her dancing. Now the music spoke to her with the ease of familiarity and all the joy that the last term had brought. She danced with all the happiness welling up inside – Mummy and Daddy watching, a proper family Easter to enjoy together, and all their new friends from Four Winds all around them. The choir sang better than ever before. For a moment, as the hall filled with song, Amanda remembered singing on the night of the power-cut, down in the kitchen. How long ago that seemed! They had sung loudly enough then to drown out poor Meena's cries as she stood at the front door. Now she was part of the school, singing along with the rest of them.

Matron looked approvingly at everyone's smart turn-out: not an unpolished shoe or an untidy hairstyle among them. The school looked splendid, and every girl was well on the way to holding a full First Aid certificate and would start to work on Home Nursing skills next term.

Further along the row, Father Higgins relaxed and enjoyed himself. He and Canis had bounded up to the school with their usual energy, even though it had been a busy morning with hospital visits, two meetings and several parish calls around the village. Now both were settled comfortably, enjoying the music. Father Higgins would have been more worried if he had known that Matron had noticed that his coat needed brushing and that his cuffs were frayed. During the school holidays, she decided, she must pop in to the presbytery to make sure that all was well there.

Father Higgin's sister, Mrs Carruthers, Amy's mother, sat next to him glowing with pride. She and her husband clutched hands when Amy marched on with the rest of the choir. How well and strong she looked! And how good to see her beaming and singing.

Shelley's grandmother was sitting next to the Brown twins'

Grandma, who had soon introduced her to the rest of the family. She looked on with pride as Shelley sang with the others in the choir. Standing next to each other, Shelley and Elizabeth were friends as they had always been, but both had a new confidence and were among a host of new friends, some of them from different countries. When she had rushed up to greet her grandmother before the concert, Shelley's talk had been of horses and cookery, sport and new friends. She had introduced Gabriele from Austria and Meena from India, with chatter and handshakes and evident confidence and goodwill. Life was evidently offering her a great deal more than hanging round the shopping centre playing truant.

Mr and Mrs Deva, sitting with a number of their relations, glowed as Renu and Meena took part in the various concert events. Watching them, the Deva parents whispered to each other. They had been right to allow Meena to join Renu here. The girls were doing well and the school was everything they had wanted for them.

As the concert ended, Aunt Win came forward to speak. Unknown to her, the girls had collected together to give her a huge bunch of flowers, and Alison now walked across to hand them to her. Everyone broke into warm applause. In a short speech Alison said how much they all owed to Mrs Ontwin and how proud every pupil was to belong to Four Winds School. This brought more applause, and then Jeannie piped up without really meaning to, 'Three Cheers for Four Winds!' and everyone gave them very heartily and clapped until their hands were tingling. Aunt Win had to wait until all the noise died down before she could make her speech.

She explained how the school had come from small beginnings to this great day, and about its plans for the future. 'As you know, it was all a mistake,' she said. 'I never meant to start a school. I just planned to take in a few pupils for a short time, and two of them were my own nieces. But it has grown and grown. After meetings with the newly-created Board of Governors, I can now safely say that we are well on the way to a sound future. We'll certainly be opening again for the summer term and for a new school year in September!' Here there were more cheers. 'And,' she went on, 'this is all due to my wonderful staff, for whom no praise is too great ...' she listed them each by name to deafening applause 'and to the girls themselves. We've weathered a burglary, a broken toe and news of an adventure in Africa. I can report that we have six new pupils arriving next term, three as boarders and three as day-girls. There will be full examinations at the end of the summer term and the girls will also be obtaining qualifications in cookery, First Aid, ballet and music, to say nothing of taking part in sporting matches of various kinds. Four Winds School is definitely on its way!'

She made some announcements about next term. Shelley was to be appointed Games Captain. Her grandmother glowed with pride. Gabriele and Elizabeth were both to be prefects. And Meena was to be special monitor in charge of the day-girls. All these girls were given special badges and reminded that they would have to take their duties seriously next term.

Then they all rose to sing the school song. All the audience had been given the words too, so the place fairly rang with the sound. From Mr and Mrs Drummond, standing next to Matron, down to Renu and Meena's cousins, brought along to get a foretaste of the school they'd be attending next year, everyone present joined in.

And then the girls marched off the platform and helped to organise tables for tea. Everyone had so much to say and there were many more introductions to be made. Alison introduced Andrew Darrington to her parents, who were soon chatting to Mrs Darrington and to Susie. 'You must bring Alison over to us for tea during the holidays,' Mrs Darrington said. 'Susie would like to hear more about Four Winds from the Head Girl herself.' Alison blushed as Andrew gave her a warm grin. He had obviously made this suggestion to his mother. She found her heart thumping as she heard her mother say 'Yes, that would be lovely' and knew that she was certainly going to see more of this tall, well-mannered and brave young man.

There were lots of other plans for the holidays too. Gabriele was keen to have as many of her friends visit her in Austria as she could. 'There is plenty of room, and the family is so large already a few more don't matter!' and Meena,

Shelley and Elizabeth were already planning a get-together at the Deva's house to make sure that the Four Winds spirit kept going locally during the holidays.

Small Amy would be busy in the holidays too, with Joan Hurry. The Carruthers were chatting to Mrs Hurry and Father Higgins grinned as he saw his small niece, once so shy and quiet, busy with Joan and Matron at the well-spread tea-table. He himself was busy talking to everyone. Parents were pleased that their girls were learning Latin – and even finding it fun – and were also glad to meet the priest whose influence on the school was an inspiring and cheering one.

Tea was a prolonged meal. The cakes and sandwiches were excellent and served with the usual Four Winds style. Then most of the girls wanted to show family and friends around, to see the music room and comfortable upstairs sitting-room and the glorious views from all the windows to the horses in the nearby meadow in one direction and out across the swimming pool and patio to the gardens in another.

Then there was all the fun of packing up cars, calling good-byes and leaving last-minutes messages. Aunt Win and Uncle Harry found they had to shake hundreds of hands as people spilled out into the cool evening, still talking and excited, with the girls' red berets bobbing about as they darted to and fro, and with bursts of friendly laughter as goodbyes were said or plans were made to meet in the holidays.

'Four Winds has made its mark locally,' Mr Deva told Aunt Win as he shook her hand. 'This concert has put the school on the map and from today everyone will know about the school. My girls are already excited about next term.'

And the next, and the next, because Four Winds is still thriving. All this happened only a short while ago, and if you go to the village today – it's not far from Mentlesham, with good road and rail connections with London – you'll see Four Winds and its pupils. On any ordinary weekday you'll see some of the day-girls at a local bus-stop, distinctive in their red and grey-blue uniforms, talking and laughing. Perhaps on a Sunday morning you'd catch a glimpse of a neat crocodile of red-hatted girls wending its way to church. At the house itself, you'd find a friendly welcome. There'd probably be a good smell of freshly brewed coffee and, if it's cold, a fire in the hearth and some girls chatting around it. Almost certainly there'd be a piano playing, somebody practising ballet somewhere, people busy in the kitchen and horses grazing in the meadow at the back. You'd hear different languages being spoken and see notices about sports events hanging in the hall, some with 'Well done!' scrawled across them where there'd been another splendid victory.

Of course, it's not always just fun, although there almost always seems to be lots of laughter and chat in the kitchen as cakes are baked or a new casserole is tried out. Upstairs there is always quiet orderliness in the schoolroom area, and everything is fresh, well-aired and tidy in all the bedrooms. If it isn't, Matron McMurdoch will always ensure that whoever is responsible gets busy to see that the room is cleaned and tidied at once!

If you ask the girls about the school, you'll find it hard to get a word in edgeways as they all tell you about it. Whatever their feelings about the different lessons and activities – not everyone enjoys the same things – they all find life at Four Winds exciting, and their eyes sparkle when they tell you about riding or dancing or First Aid, or even something crazy like Latin spelling competitions.

There are still lots of good things to come and more adventures. This was the school that started by accident. 'I never really meant to start a school,' Aunt Win still says sometimes.